DRAGON BIKE

FANTASTICAL STORIES OF BICYCLING, FEMINISM, AND DRAGONS

EDITED BY

ELLY BLUE

MICROCOSM PUBLISHING

PORTLAND, OR

DRAGON BIKE
FANTASTICAL STORIES OF BICYCLING, FEMINISM, AND DRAGONS

Edited by Elly Blue
All content © its creators, 2020
Final editorial content © Elly Blue, 2020
This edition © Elly Blue Publishing, an imprint of Microcosm Publishing, 2020
First printing, February 10, 2020
All work remains the property of the original creators.

ISBN 978-1-62106-047-5
This is Microcosm #274

Elly Blue Publishing, an imprint of Microcosm Publishing
2752 N Williams Ave.
Portland, OR 97227

Cover art by Cecila Granata | www.ceciliagranata.com
Inside cover art by Tessa Hulls
Book Design by Joe Biel
Special thanks to Tomy Huynh and Cynthia Marts for editorial assistance

Elly Blue Publishing, an imprint of Microcosm Publishing
2752 N Williams Ave
Portland, OR 97227

This is Bikes in Space Volume 6
For more volumes visit BikesInSpace.com
For more feminist bicycle books and zines visit TakingTheLane.com

If you bought this on Amazon, I'm so sorry because you could have gotten it cheaper and supported a small, independent publisher at MicrocosmPublishing.com

To join the ranks of high-class stores that feature Microcosm titles, talk to your local rep: In the U.S. **Como** (Atlantic), **Fujii** (Midwest), **Travelers West** (Pacific), **Brunswick** in Canada, **Turnaround** in Europe, **New South** in Australia and New Zealand, and **Baker & Taylor Publisher Services** in Asia, India, and South Africa.

Library of Congress Cataloging-in-Publication Data
Names: Blue, Elly, author.
Title: Dragon bike : fantastical stories of bicycling, feminism, and
 dragons / Elly Blue.
Description: Portland, OR : Microcosm Publishing, 2020. | Summary: "A
 collection of short stories that are about feminism, bikes and
 dragons"-- Provided by publisher.
Identifiers: LCCN 2019020213 | ISBN 9781621060475 (paperback)
Subjects: LCSH: Cycling--Fiction. | Feminism--Fiction. | Dragons--Fiction.
 | GSAFD: Fantasy fiction.
Classification: LCC PS3602.L836 A6 2020 | DDC 813/.6--dc23
LC record available at https://lccn.loc.gov/2019020213

[TABLE OF CONTENTS]

INTRODUCTION

The week I moved to Portland, Oregon in 2001, I stepped onto my college quad one night into a maelstrom of fire-breathing bicycles. Jousting knights faced off, perched precariously on mutant bicycles, welded double-high or with six-foot long forks. Intoxicated combatants in ramshackle armor were steadied by their squires, who handed them lances and lit the padded ends on fire. With a great roar, they rode at each other, lances, bikes, and sometimes costumes aflame, firecrackers blasting behind them into the crowd. Beer cans flew, music blared and the crowd milled and jumped. I was overwhelmed, excited, and strangely soothed. The lawlessness of the experience matched something inside me, even though a reflexive disapproval kept me on the sidelines.

Later, I learned this fiery display was engineered by post-apocalyptic bicycle club C.H.V.N.K. 666, a joyous uprising from the rubble of industry and civilization, building steeds out of garbage and directing their despair and fury into glorious explosions of creativity and destruction like the rally I'd stumbled into. In their worldview, the dragons of capitalism had already laid waste to our world and there was nothing to do but lovingly battle each other in the ruins.

I chose the theme for this volume not purely out of commercial impulse, even though the finale of *Game of Thrones* had yet to fizzle disappointingly into existence and leave fans wishing for a different outcome to all those stories, especially the women's. I had it in mind, of course, but I also thought about the Pern novels I escaped into as a girl. I thought about roaring, orange-faced demagogues, their golden towers and hoarded wealth. I thought about the fire-engulfed bicyclists and roaring crowd who shook me out of my shell that night in Portland, and the extreme gender imbalance of that scene occurred to me for the first time. I wanted a different outcome to that story, too—one where I'd showed up the next week and learned to weld, and turned my own drunken energy into a public expression of mayhem and metaphor.

The point of this *Bikes in Space* series is to encourage people to revise the fantasies that inform our culture. In this sixth volume of the series, we're tackling one of the most meaningful and intense mythologies there is.

The dragons in today's massive media franchises most closely resemble the dragon of Beowulf, a giant, winged fire-breathing lizard who was slain by two lone knights after terrorizing the townspeople in revenge for a cup stolen from its hoard. In Han and Qing Dynasty China, dragons were wingless serpents that brought rain and good luck. The emperors identified themselves as their descendants, and anyone else wearing or displaying a dragon image would be executed. In ancient Mayan lore, Q'uq'umatz was a feathered serpent who created the world and ruled the wind and rain. To the old Sufi poet Rumi, a dragon represented human greed and lust, an evil creature that must be fought. The ancient Egyptian Apep was a giant, serpentine chaos deity who did regular battle with the sun god Ra. Someone I met at a convention once looked deeply into my eyes and told me that the existence of dragon legends around the world proves that dinosaurs walked the earth in relatively recent memory and thus the creation story of Genesis was a documentary account. Of all these, the image I always come back to is the one in *Tehanu*, Ursula K. Leguin's attempt to turn the Tolkien-esque dragon myth on its head—instead of a violent hoarder of wealth, her dragon rises from the ashes of trauma, and chooses a quiet village life instead of a glorious one of swooping through the skies.

Dragon stories are a powerful force in our world. I love the way the contributors in this book have chosen to engage with dragons. Some are great beasts of destruction, like in "Slow Burn, Steady Flame" and "The Mothers of Pequeño Lago." Others represent joyful ways to bring play and meaning back into life—like in "'Round" and "Chen D'Angelo and the Chinese-Italian Dragon" or Tessa Hulls' illustration on the inside covers of this book. In some of these stories, dragons are reinvented entirely: in "The Beasts of Bataranam" they symbolize resistance against colonial oppression, and in "Wyvern" and "The Sounds of Home," they have become something disquietingly futuristic and new.

Some of these stories are disturbing; others are adorable; some show dragons (and people) at their most terrible and others show them at their most kind. I hope you enjoy them all as much as I did.

–Elly Blue
Portland, Oregon
August, 2019

CHEN D'ANGELO AND THE CHINESE-ITALIAN DRAGON

Jennifer Lee Rossman

The mural on the pizzeria wall shows a Chinese dragon weaving between Ionic columns in a fantastical landscape of misty mountains and Tuscan vineyards. His frills and furs, the colors of the Italian flag, fan out like whirling dresses, but that's not the part that transfixes me. It's the sun, represented by a little orange circle, half-hidden by the mountains as it paints the clouds vibrant pinks and yellows.

The only sun I've ever seen doesn't actually move across the sky, since it's just a really big lightbulb stretching from one end of the ship to the other, but it does turn a nice sunsetty red for a few minutes before it shuts off for the night. It's the only sun Mama Giulia has ever seen, too, but she painted this mural with a real sun, the kind my kids and grandkids will have when the ship gets to our new home.

Sometimes I forget this isn't real, that this isn't the only way humanity ever lived.

Anything you want, the *Belinda* has it. You want to live in a city? She's got one the size of Manhattan, all shiny skyscrapers and neon lights, packed full of stores, movie theaters, and thirty-seven pizza shops. Yes, really. I counted. But only Xiang & Giulia's is any good. Best Italian restaurant in all of Chinatown, and I'm not just saying that because my moms own it.

Or maybe country life is more your style. *Belinda* has farmland aplenty, all nurtured by the artificial sunlight running down the central axis of her cylindrical shape. Forests and bike paths full of wildlife from around the world complete the outdoorsy effect.

Seriously. You name it, she's got it. Big library like in *Beauty & the Beast*? Yep. Gender health clinic? Several. Rollercoaster? It's called La Requin and it will absolutely make you puke.

There's just one thing (besides sunsets, I mean) that it doesn't have: myths.

See, *Belinda* is a generation ship, hurtling through space somewhere between Earth and the promise of a new home. Earth was dying, so humanity had to leave. Back when my grandparents were kids, they packed up everything they'd need to start over on another planet.

Except I think something got left behind. I think in their rush to pack all the horses and DVDs and medicine, they forgot to bring the gods and monsters and miracles. I imagine a sad little suitcase full of myths, all alone on the launchpad.

Sure, we have stories, and people still pray, but I don't think we believe as much as we used to. There's nothing on this ship we didn't put here, no hidden pockets that haven't been explored. The water in the lakes and rivers came from bottles, not magic springs full of mermaids, and I think someone would have noticed by now if there was a lake monster on the shipping manifest.

And now we're going to lose our dragon.

Mama Xiang walks in from the kitchen, carrying a tray of drinks to the one table that isn't empty tonight. She pauses as she passes me, taking in the dejected slump of my shoulders as I stare at the mural behind the counter. "We'll be okay, Chen," she assures me, stooping to kiss the top of my head.

It should bother me that we're going to lose the restaurant if we can't make rent. It should bother me that our little slice of the city is going to get a little less unique, that our few regulars are going to have to find some other place that serves Sichuan garlic knots.

But it's the dragon that bothers me, because we need magic in our lives. We need to remember what it was like not to know everything.

I look down at my tablet and my homework assignment: an essay about my choice of Gliese 581g's extinct creatures. Mankind hasn't even set foot on the planet, but we already have volumes written about its history. The probes and rovers have explored every inch of it, even going so far as to dig up its fossils. There will be nothing left to wonder when we get there.

What if we forget how?

• • •

There's this forest on the edge of the city. Oaks and cypresses and baobabs, moose and red pandas and pangolins all living together to form one impossible ecosystem. It's like you took all of Earth's forests and condensed them into a few thousand acres.

Even though someone chose all the animals and landscaped the hills and valleys, some parts of the forest have rearranged themselves. Sure, there are a lot of places where everything gets along, but in other places, plants and animals from the same habitat have found each other, creating little ecosystems all their own. Pitcher plants and sphagnum moss grow in the wetlands, lemurs and parrots live where the humidity makes the air feel like liquid . . .

The forest is the one place on the *Belinda* that feels really wild and magical to me, like the wilderness of old Earth. If there were a dragon hiding on this ship, it would be right here.

My best friend Georgia isn't so sure.

"Trust me," I say as we walk our bikes up a well-packed dirt path leading away from the city. "This is going to work."

She reads my lips and shakes her head, pausing and leaning her silver bike against her hip to respond in sign. "*Adults are smart. They won't fall for it.*"

"Adults," I correct, "will fall for anything if they think it's their idea. Now come on."

We get on our bikes and pedal deeper into the woods. Georgia can't sign with both hands occupied, but we don't have much time before school starts. We come to the swampy part where some of the older kids swear they've seen crocodiles lurking beneath the thick, green water.

Supposedly, the only crocodiles on board are frozen embryos in labs. The *Belinda* is a huge ship, but not big enough to guarantee predators and humans won't come into contact, so people carefully control the herbivore population. The carnivores will be thawed out when we get to Gliese.

But that doesn't stop people from whispering about the disgruntled scientist who did it early and let them loose in the woods, and we're going to use these rumors to our advantage.

We stop where weeds start to encroach on the path. I find a pile of shiny black poop and pump my fist in victory.

Georgia laughs at my excitement. "*I have some dog poop at home you can have.*"

"We're still visible from the main path," I explain, "but secluded enough for deer—and dragons—to come through." I motion for her to open her backpack while I do the same. Nestled between my tablet and art projects is some shed dragon skin I made from napkins and dried glue, with some spices mixed in for color and texture.

"*Nice,*" Georgia signs. She has bits of red fur from an old stuffed animal, and we spread it liberally around the area. It looks a little cheesy, but we're ten. We're not special effects artists.

And anyway, the fur and skin is just to get people's attention. We hide the good evidence a little deeper, making big scratches with our house keys on trees and pressing claw marks into the soft earth.

We stand back and look at our work. I'm no expert, but it looks good to me. Not too obvious to be a hoax, but obvious enough to be noticed.

I turn to Georgia. "What do you think?"

She gives a tentative thumbs-up.

·   ·   ·

I think it's going to work. I spent all recess planting the seeds of a new urban legend, and even invited some kids to go bike riding later in the week; just in case no one discovers our evidence, I'll lead them right to it. And Georgia has put out the word that my mothers are experts in folklore in case anyone needs help researching a project.

Within a few days, the whole ship will be abuzz with talk of dragons, and people will start coming into the pizzeria and—

My good mood fizzles away the instant I walk into the restaurant.

Mama Giulia is crying. She hides it well, keeping her face toward the wall as she slices a white ricotta pizza on shaobing dough that peppers the air with a thick sesame aroma, but she's breathing fast and she isn't humming. That's my perpetually upbeat Mama G's version of sobbing.

"What's wrong?" I ask, setting my backpack on the counter.

"I'll tell you later."

The fact that she doesn't bother lying to me sends a jolt of dread straight to my heart, and I rush through the swinging doors to the kitchen. Mama Xiang has her face in her hands, her elbows leaning heavily on the prep table.

"Mama?" I say quietly. The sight of my heroes, the strongest women I've ever met, reduced to tears is more upsetting than whatever they're crying about.

Mama Xiang doesn't look up. "We're being evicted."

I frown. "I know. Mr. B. told us he isn't renewing our lease, but if we can raise the money—"

"No, baby. Not at the end of the month." She looks at me, her face wet and hollow. "He's moving the date up. We're closing tomorrow."

My mouth hangs open in shock. No. We were supposed to have more time. We were supposed to be able to scrounge together enough to pay for the next month and by then, the dragon hoax would have brought people in. Maybe not a lot, but enough of them would discover a love of hoisin and marinara and become regulars. Enough that we could manage rent every month.

My eyes flick out the door, to the mural painted on the wall above our few customers. What will replace it? Will the new owners cover it with a gaudy logo for a fitness center or shelves full of designer clothing? Will they just slash some white paint over it and let it be forgotten?

"We'll be okay," Mama Xiang says, but I don't think she believes it. "We own the apartment outright, and Giulia and I can get jobs at other restaurants. She's the best chef on this ship. We'll be okay."

• • •

I sit on the roof of our apartment in the Little Italy district, watching the sun begin its red phase, and I know we won't be okay.

The pizzeria is my home as much as the apartment is. It's where I go to do homework while my moms cook and sing and tell stories their grandmas told them about Earth.

It's the one place on all of the *Belinda* that smells like anise and basil, where you can hear tarantella music played on a paixiao flute.

It is the only place that has a Chinese-Italian dragon on the wall and that makes it special because, while the ship is so diverse and amazing, the city is much like the forest. You can mix all the plants and animals together and they live in harmony but sometimes they thrive best unincorporated. Where the pitcher plants and the moss and the little peep toads preserve and share their environment because they share a common evolutionary history.

That's why we have Chinatown, and why we have Little Italy, but my history doesn't fit so easily into just one section of the city. My name is Chen D'Angelo. I have Italian coloring and Chinese features. Part of me doesn't fit no matter where I go, but I'm complete at Xiang and Giulia's.

So I need to save it, and I need to do it tonight.

I call Georgia on my way downstairs; her smiling face appears as a hologram in front of me a moment later.

"Can you meet me on the bike trail in half an hour?"

She frowns. "*Say again?*"

I take a deep breath and try to talk slower so she can read my lips, but I'm so excited and anxious and I just want to babble. "Can you meet me on the bike trail? We need to make people believe in dragons, and we need to do it tonight."

Georgia opens her mouth in surprise but nods and signs, *"Meet you there."*

"Bring fabric," I say. "Flowy skirts, long jackets . . . anything red, white, and green. And put out the word that there's something roaming the woods. Start a hashtag, if you have to. We need as many people as possible to go dragon hunting tonight."

"Got it." She waves and hangs up.

"Mamas!" I say as I rush into our apartment. "We still own it tonight, right?"

They look up from the kitchen table where they've been poring over bills. Mama Giulia rubs her face wearily. "What are you talking about, Chen?"

"The restaurant!" I go into my room and start pulling out any piece of flowy clothing I own, stuffing it into my backpack. "Is it still ours? Can we still sell food?"

"Until tomorrow." Mama Xiang stands, her arms crossed in concern as she watches me. "Why?"

"And if we earn enough money to pay the rent tonight, do you think Mr. B. will let us keep it?"

She looks bewildered by the idea, but nods. "He wants money; if we can pay him as much as the new tenants would, I don't think he'll care who he gets it from."

That's what I was hoping she'd say. I go back to the kitchen, eyeing the tablecloth. It's white and lacy and ruffled, with stripes of green and red on the edges. It would flutter spectacularly in the wind.

"Can I borrow this?" I ask, carefully transferring their paperwork to the counter.

"Chen!" Mama Giulia's voice is firm, but not mad. Just exhausted by everything around her. "What are you doing?"

I wrap my arms around her, then around Mama X. "I have an idea. Just trust me, and go make mini bok choy pizzas. As many as you can." I whisk the tablecloth away with a flourish. "I'm bringing friends."

·   ·   ·

The sun has gone into moon mode by the time I meet up with Georgia, the sky a starless black with only a dim, silvery light to see by. The forest is alive with sound; I know there aren't any predators out here, but the hairs on the back of my neck still stand on end and I'm glad my bike has a headlight.

Georgia is waiting for me near the swamp. Her four siblings have come with her, all of them laden with fabric that stands out starkly in the simulated moonlight.

"We called everyone," she signs, holding her hands in the beam of my light.

"Even Uncle Liam," her older brother adds. "He's . . ."

"An interesting character," Georgia supplies. *"Definitely believes in the alligator story and will drag all his friends along with him."*

"And it's trending on BelindaChat," one of her sisters reports, looking at her phone.

Perfect.

The first people show up just as we're finishing preparation; I can hear them whispering and see their lights bobbing through the trees. I look over my shoulder.

"Ready?"

Georgia and her family give me enthusiastic thumbs-ups, and their heads disappear under the fabric to become humps on our dragon's back. I pull my own head beneath the tablecloth, and we begin pedaling.

Down the path we go, picking up speed until we whip past the monster hunters, who let out yelps of surprise. We might not look like much standing still, but our sheets and skirts flutter in the wind and obscure the fact that we're just six kids on bikes. We're a forty-foot-long dragon.

We loop around and make another pass by the people in the woods, then disappear down a rarely used bike path and hide behind a rocky outcropping, where we shed our costume and wait. I have to clap my hand over my mouth to keep from giggling as the adrenaline and excitement runs through my body.

When the monster hunters finally catch up to us, we're just six terrified kids on bikes.

"It was a dragon!" I say, pretending to hyperventilate. "A big one!"

Georgia signs so fast, I almost can't keep up. *"It had a fuzzy mane and long tail. It floated over the ground."*

We point in a random direction and off they go in search of the dragon. We don our costume and take a shortcut around their path, and are waiting for them a quarter mile down the trail. Shouts go up at the sight of us.

We repeat this charade all night, and the crowd following us grows larger. Some of them must have realized what's going on, but no one tries to stop it.

When it seems like the entire ship is running after us, all laughing and whooping, we don't even pretend anymore. We just stop our bikes and uncover our heads, the dragon's fluttering furs draped around our shoulders.

"It was headed into town!" I shout, and we take off again, my headlight leading the way as our strange procession twines its way out of the forest and through city streets. More people join us as we pass by them, drawn in by the joy bubbling off of us.

I think they've all remembered what it's like to believe. Not just in dragons, but in mystery and the excitement of discovery. And as we enter Chinatown and the glowing paper lanterns of Xiang and Giulia's appear up ahead, I hope everyone will enjoy discovering our little pizzeria with the Chinese-Italian dragon on the wall.

WITCHCANIX

M. Lopes da Silva

Marlo muttered a few brief words to wake the spell up and applied the tip of the runic torch to the alicorn femur. A prismatic scattering of sparks reflected in her black safety visor and the femur glowed a dull red. Quickly, Marlo joined the bone to the rest of the bicycle frame.

Marlo grimaced as she worked. Witchcanix, her shop, had seven days left. Seven days to fulfill the Queen's order, and they didn't even have a dragon to work with. She could only fill her hours with busywork, and hope that the Queen wasn't in a beheading mood.

"Hey! I got it! I got it!"

Marlo couldn't hear the excited shout above the dull roar of the chop shop, but she soon saw the grease-smeared face of her assistant, bobbing just beyond the edge of the worktable. Marlo cut the spell feed to the torch with a sigh and flipped up her safety visor.

"I told you not to stand over there when I'm working at the table. And where are your goggles?"

Betula rolled her eyes. "I just came here to give you the absolute best news in the multiverse, and you're talking about goggles!"

Marlo sniffed. "New eyes are expensive. And you go through a pair a month."

"At *least*," Betula replied with a grin. "Come on, what's been the worst, most awful thing going on in your life right now?"

Marlo arched a lone eyebrow.

"The worst thing? Are you talking about the Queen's order?"

"Yep," Betula nodded.

"Well now," Marlo smiled, pulling off her heavy, basilisk leather gloves and flexing her fingers. "Why didn't you say so?"

• • •

Marlo studied the dragon's corpse with a frown. It was the right size, with a beautiful emerald green color fading to a fine yellow along wing webbing softer than bat leather. She chewed on the inside of her cheek as she walked around the magnificent dead beast.

"You said you bought it from Sir Witlow?" she asked. "I told you not to deal with that creep."

Betula scratched the back of her neck. "I know, Marlo, but we were running out of options. None of the other knights had any dragons on hand. And I saw his license and everything—his paperwork was legit."

Marlo ran her hands over the dragon's flank. The corpse was still warm; dragons didn't start cooling for a good seventy-two hours after death. At least there weren't any obvious signs that the dragon had been illegally poached—no jewels embedded in the scales. The Cognizant, the magical non-human beings that were officially recognized as self-aware, and therefore granted legal protections, liked to wear decorative gems.

She clucked her tongue in frustration. Sir Witlow had once sold her a unicorn he'd claimed had died of natural causes, but once Marlo had begun to convert the animal into a custom-ordered mecha suit, a magical plague had been released into the chop shop. The costly damage had almost shut down the shop for good. She still found hobgoblins in the plumbing, and hadn't been able to afford replacing the metal press.

Marlo sighed. "Well, it doesn't look illegal, in any case. He had a dragon-slaying permit signed by the *current* Queen?"

Betula nodded. "With a wax seal and everything. Want me to get the body to one of the scissor lifts?"

Marlo patted the flank of the dead dragon. "Yeah. Let's be respectful and get a blessing going around number eight. I'll be in my office confirming the runes."

"You got it, Marlo."

• • •

Three witches in Marlo's coven handled the dissection as she supervised. The cutting and sorting took half the night. Bleary-eyed, most of the witches left to go home and sleep, but Marlo stayed behind. She was awake with the electric itch that she just couldn't shake once she started a project. Her mind kept going back to the dragon.

It was easily Marlo's most ambitious project to date. The Queen wanted a custom bicycle for the Galaxy Royale, the race that just about everyone across the eighteen kingdoms enthusiastically followed every spring. The grand prize this year was a rare Phantom Pegasus, made by the great Angela Sanchez over five thousand years ago, and still running in mint condition.

Marlo had studied, but never attempted, spectral engineering. The ghosts had a tendency to leak out and haunt things. But the Phantom Pegasus was a gorgeous, solidly built bicycle with gear-rigged wings that produced magical uplift—a feat of witch engineering that had not been reproduced successfully for centuries. Marlo wanted desperately to study the Phantom Pegasus up close, so she had been building her own alicorn from scratch; to give herself an edge in the upcoming race.

But the Queen wanted a dragon bike—dragons were known for converting into some of the lightest, fastest, and finest mechanical pieces around. Their bones were both lightweight and incredibly strong, but finicky to work with. The runic torch setting had to be extremely high, and you had to go slow. Any damage along the way meant scrapping the work and starting over from the beginning, and there was only a finite amount of dragon to work with.

Marlo picked up some of the glittering emerald scales. She wanted to honor the dragon and convert its body into something worthy of its former occupant. She put down the scales and returned to her notebook, full of sketches and endless notes.

This was it; her opportunity to make something fantastic.

·　　·　　·

Marlo labored by the lifts for days, stopping only for the brief breaks that her own body demanded. She ate, she slept, she built the dragon.

Betula was Marlo's second set of hands, capably adjusting and tweaking and building along the way. Betula was sloppy about her own safety, but performed fastidious work. Marlo was proud, once more, of her assistant's grace at the bench.

"This is going to be amazing," Betula said, her mouth half-loaded with egg salad sandwich. "I've never seen a bike like this before. Her Royal Highness is going to skunk you in the race."

Marlo shrugged, swallowing a slug of cold tea. "Then I'll get to see the Phantom Pegasus in the royal garage. Same thing to me."

Betula shook her head. "Man, you really love spectral engineering. Why don't you try and build something in a corner of the shop? You could have my bench if you wanted space."

Marlo shook her head. "If we got ghosts in here, that would be it for this place. I can't afford to replace any of the major equipment right now. It's not fair to everybody to keep a pet project like that around here."

Betula frowned. "Is it that bad? Maybe we could pitch in and help you with the lease for a couple months—"

Marlo scowled. "No! Not happening. If this place goes under, it's only taking me with it. You're the best coven I've ever had and I'm not putting you all at risk."

Betula blinked, her eyes suddenly damp. "You big dummy!"

"You're not stopping me," Marlo replied, taking a bite of her oatcake. "If the banks collect, they'll want magic as collateral. They can have mine. Yours shouldn't be in jeopardy."

Betula shook her head. "You're so talented! It would be awful if they . . ."

"They won't," Marlo said, pointing at the dragon in front of them, a half-built, towering, skeletal frame. "Look at that! The Queen's going to love it. And the rest of the coven is finishing the Duke's order. We'll make the rent this month, and the next. We can even start thinking about repairing the unicorn drill."

Betula stared at the dragon and let herself be persuaded.

•   •   •

It was when they had to apply the activation spell that they ran into trouble.

Marlo double- and triple-checked the task list that morning. Betula even humored her by wearing her safety goggles. The quartz wand was connected to the dragon skull, the spell was verbally activated, and then the lights went out.

"Did we blow a fuse?" Betula wondered aloud.

"I don't think so," Marlo replied, touching the smooth, polished surface of the skull. Suddenly she flinched, drawing her hands away from it. The skull had grown very hot, very quickly.

"There's something wrong—" Marlo began to say, but then the dragon bike lit up with a searing pale flame and a tremendous roar echoed through the chop shop.

Marlo and Betula clutched their ears, trying to suppress the hideous, painful sound, but soon they realized that the roar persisted within their heads regardless of their efforts. The roar was being directly projected into their minds.

"Why is the dragon's atomic constellation so upset?" Betula groaned.

"It shouldn't be!" Marlo growled. "I compensated for constellation hinges. I even baked in an emergency oversoul release!"

WHAT HAVE YOU DONE?

Marlo and Betula stared at each other, stunned. The growling, raspy voice still echoed in their minds.

"I'm going to hex that knight *right now*!"

"Marlo! Wait! Hexing costs too much!" Betula winced, grappling with Marlo's arms as Marlo tried to grab her wand in the dark.

"He sold me one of the Cognizant! I'm going to lose everything!"

WHAT INJUSTICE IS THIS, PETTY MORTALS?

"I could be beheaded! Beheaded, Betula!" Marlo bellowed.

LET THE BEHEADING COMMENCE, FOUL MURDERERS!

"Hey!" Marlo shouted, turning to the bike. "Hey! We didn't kill you! It was that creepo Sir Witlow!"

I CARE NOT FOR YOUR FINGER-POINTING.

Marlo went limp, much to Betula's relief.

"I'm going to die because of a stupid knight. In about . . . four hours. That's when I'm going to die."

I LOOK FORWARD TO YOUR DEATH, AND MY RETURN TO MY PROPER FORM.

"Oh," Betula said, turning to the luminescent bicycle frame. "That's not going to be possible, I'm sorry."

. . . WHAT?

Marlo explained everything.

• • •

The dragon was silent for a long while. In that silence, Marlo began to wonder if there was anything she should do before her imminent death. She had just decided to start sorting out the paperwork in the office when the dragon spoke.

WHAT DO I LOOK LIKE?

"Oh, you're beautiful," Betula said. "Marlo poured her heart out into designing you. You're two stories tall, the pedals operate your wings, and your bones are buffed up like mirrors."

CAN I FLY?

"No," Marlo said reluctantly, "the wings are just decorative. Only spectral engineering can produce the kind of wings you're talking about."

GIVE ME THOSE WINGS, MORTAL.

"I can't," Marlo said. "The last person who knew how to make them died over four thousand years ago. I was hoping to learn how by examining the Phantom Pegasus."

THE PRIZE YOU SEEK?

"That's the one," Betula said.

THEN I SHALL WIN THE PRIZE, AND REGAIN MY POWERS OF FLIGHT IN THIS IGNOBLE FORM!

"Good luck figuring that one out. I'll be in pieces in a pine box," Marlo replied.

"Marlo's the best witchcanic I know," Betula said suddenly, "she's probably the only one who could figure out how the Phantom Pegasus works."

THEN WE MUST KEEP THIS WRETCHED MORTAL ALIVE. BUT THE KNIGHT SHALL KNOW MY WRATH!

Marlo sat upright, eyeing Betula sidelong. "We could help you sort out the knight. But you'd have to do us a favor, first."

DO NOT ATTEMPT TO TRICK ME, MORTAL!

Marlo shook her head. "No trick here, but I need you to make sure that you don't say anything in front of the Queen. The minute you say a word in front of her, she'll know that you were one of the Cognizant, and I'll be beheaded. That's the law."

I SHALL CONSIDER YOUR FAVOR. GO NOW.

The lights came back on. Marlo and Betula squinted and sucked air between their teeth at the sudden brightness. The frame of the dragon bicycle shone brilliantly underneath the abrupt electric glow.

· · ·

From a distance, Marlo and Betula watched the queen approach on her copper hippogryph. The whirring feather blades made the dust in the fields swirl and tumble. As she descended, the copper horse hooves of the landing gear pawed the earth below.

REMEMBER YOUR PROMISE, MORTALS.

Betula quickly slipped her hand into Marlo's and gave it a reassuring squeeze. Marlo smiled grimly.

"I'll get you your wings, dragon, and your justice," she said. "That's a witch's vow."

THEN I AM SATISFIED.

And she was.

THE SOUND OF HOME

Monique Cuillerier

Evelyn sat in front of the environmental controls, as she did every night. At some point, she would nod off, the daily grip of anxiety and resignation loosening as exhaustion overtook her.

She sat with her eyes fixed on the control panel. The internal atmosphere reading was green, the mix of nitrogen, oxygen, argon, and trace gases close to that of Earth. She worried that something would happen and she wouldn't be able to fix it. The thought of the hostile atmosphere seeping into the locus, their base here on Enceladus, rested inside her as both a fear and an end of fear.

There was no sound other than the occasional hum or beep from the controls. Evelyn had been born on Earth and grown up there. No matter how long she spent away, on Mars, and then Titan, and now here, she missed the sounds of home: water and wind, the buzz of insects. Inside the locus or on a ship, the mechanical noises were not the same.

Her fingers lay near the panel while she began the nightly ritual of allowing her mind to wander back to what it was like before.

•　　　•　　　•

The dream always began at the same point.

"Zaza Evie, we need to go and see the dragons!"

Evelyn considered her child's demand. She needed to check the sensor grid anyway and, although the diagnostics could be run remotely, there was no reason why they couldn't get the bike out and take the readings directly and then Leth could see the dragons.

"Okay, but we need to check the sensors while we're there."

Leth nodded.

"Let's get ready then."

•　　　•　　　•

"Look, the dragons are waking up!"

From the path, Evelyn's eyes went in the direction Leth was pointing. The geysers at Enceladus's south pole were putting on quite the show today. While Evelyn knew that the large amount of material spewing out was because they were at the point in their orbit around Saturn where they were farthest from the planet, Leth saw only magic. Dragons inside of their moon, breathing out and feeding the E Ring.

"Let's keep going."

"That one is a baby dragon," Leth said with the certainty of a five year old, indicating a smaller, closer geyser.

"Maybe," Evelyn said, "come on."

They dismounted from the bike they shared. It wasn't a proper bike in Evelyn's mind, too sturdy, the wheels solid, and seats too wide in order to accommodate their spacesuits, but it made for convenient surface transportation, independent of external power sources.

"Here," she said to Leth, "you take the readings with your device. I'm going to measure how close that baby dragon is and see if the grid needs to be moved."

Leth went off to do as she had been asked, as if it were a game. She was the same as any child, Evelyn reassured herself. The thought had been running through her head since the report had come back from UNSpace. Evelyn was an astrobiologist and if anyone should have been able to detect a difference, it should have been her.

But neither as a scientist nor as a parent could she see the alteration that had been detected in Leth.

Integrated, they had said. *Colonized by the local bacteria. A part of the Enceladean ecosystem now.*

What did any of that really mean?

Evelyn had snapped and said maybe some good next-generation antibiotics would do the trick.

We want to see what happens. We're not sure it would even be a good idea, or safe, for Leth to leave.

Evelyn breathed deeply, trying to maintain her composure. Leth knew none of this, was too young to begin to understand what was happening. And once again, Evelyn wished that Aerin was here and not on Titan. They had spoken, of course, but she would have liked in-person help with the parenting.

That was a thought she often had while they were apart, but it came to her now, with an almost physical force, that she might never touch Aerin again.

UNSpace said that they were waiting on the last round of test results; that they were still trying to decide what to do next, that their comments were just "thinking out loud," but Evelyn's mind kept returning to the pre-departure discussions, when the possibility of coming into contact with a hostile microbial life form had been raised.

The standard operating procedure was containment. Leth—and Evelyn by default, and maybe the others here on the surface, too—were not going to be leaving.

Not for now. Perhaps not ever.

Her breath caught in her chest and she consciously took control of it, in and out, visualizing herself breathing out the anxiety clouding her mind and breathing in calm.

"Zaza, I'm done."

She spun around. Leth was only a metre away.

"Thank you," she said automatically. "Have you transmitted the results to the locus?"

"Yes."

"We can head back then. Are you hungry?"

"Hungry as a dragon!"

"Do dragons get very hungry?"

"They do," the child said with certainty. "They told me so."

Evelyn stopped.

"They told you?"

"They talk to me. And I talk back to them. They're not at all scary like you'd think from stories."

"That's good," Evelyn said and began walking again. Leth certainly was creative. "Come on, back to the bike."

"How long will it be?"

"You know how far it is."

"How long?"

"Twenty minutes."

"Tell me the story of the best and worst day," Leth demanded as they reached the bike.

"Once you're on your seat," Evelyn said, helping the child up.

Evelyn was happy that Leth showed an interest in her childhood reminisces. She got on and started pedalling.

"When I was little like you, I lived on a lake, a big body of water. It was a small town, but there were more people there than here. In the summer, when we had no school, my friends and I would spend our days however we wished. We would leave on our bikes in the morning . . ."

"Bikes like this one?"

Evelyn smiled to herself. Over time Leth's questions had become part of the story.

"Sort of like this one. But we didn't have to wear spacesuits while we pedaled, so they were smaller."

"Can we look at pictures of them when we get back?"

"Sure." Evelyn paused to make sure there were no more questions and then continued. "It was glorious. We would ride around the lake on the dirt road and stop at the beach to spend the day exploring and swimming and only leave when it was time for dinner."

"Didn't you see your zazas?"

"Not during the day, they were at work."

Even without being able to see the child behind her, Evelyn knew that there would be a frown on Leth's face as she asked, "You couldn't go with them?"

"They didn't have those sorts of jobs."

"That doesn't sound like fun."

Perhaps not fun for her parents, but it had been for Evelyn and she wouldn't have traded those long perfect summers, that last perfect summer, for anything. And what had she provided for her own child? Endless ice and, at most, a handful of people.

And genetic-level contamination that was going to preclude her from leaving.

She felt dizzy with a wave of preemptive grief.

"Zaza . . ." Leth brought her back to the present.

"Where was I?"

With a sigh, Leth said, "You were supposed to be talking about the best and worst day."

"On one of those hot and sunny and beautiful days, that started like any other, my friends and I rode our bikes to the beach like usual. We brought a picnic and we were going to be there the entire day. The entire morning we spent swimming and then we had lunch and afterwards, Kai took a nap. And Eugenie wanted to read. So, Toolika and I went off down the beach, walking at the high waterline, looking for what we could find."

Leth was entranced, as always. Evelyn had explained the beach and sun and books and picnics so many times, the whole array outside her child's experience.

"There were so many rocks and we would pick through them, one at a time. On some were fossils, sometimes very faint and other times almost like a drawing. And that day, we found a rock—it was so big, I can't believe that we had never noticed it before—and it was covered with footprints, from something like a lizard."

"An animal."

"Exactly. And I looked at the prints and I wanted to know all about who made them. I wanted to be a biologist."

"And you wanted to look for more?"

"I did," Evelyn said sadly.

"But when you got back to your home . . . " Leth prompted.

"When we got back, my zazas told me that we were leaving Earth. That we were going to be moving to the Moon."

"Did you get to take your bike with you?"

But they were back at the locus and Evelyn neglected to answer. It had always been a sore spot between her and her parents.

•   •   •

Later that night, when Evelyn should have been asleep, she instead sat on the floor beside her child's bed.

She and Leth had arrived back to find the others packing. The message from UNSpace had been what she feared. The tests were complete. Only Leth was infected, damaged, compromised, colonized—whatever you wanted to call it. Better safe than sorry, UNSpace had said, the others had to go.

But not Leth. Not now, or yet, or maybe ever.

Tears were falling from her eyes and she rocked back and forth, trying so hard to be silent.

The horrible realization came to her that she would need to explain this to Leth. Need to tell her why they were staying. Why the others were going.

•   •   •

Evelyn came awake, as she often did, still deep in that moment of recognition, her stomach twisted and anxious. She was still hunched over the environmental control display, her cheek pressed against the metal corner and hurting.

"Zaza?" Leth said from the doorway. "It's morning."

"I'm sorry," spilled out of Evelyn's mouth. "I'll get breakfast."

She shook her head and stood up unsteadily, making her way to the kitchen. It had been seven years. Seven years of reliving how they had found themselves in this situation.

"Zaza Evie?"

Evelyn turned at Leth's use of the childhood name. "Yes?"

"Yesterday, after class, I was talking with some of my friends." Leth took virtual classes with children on Titan. Evelyn looked away. "Zaza?"

Evelyn hadn't meant to tune out what she was saying, but a message alert on her device had her attention.

IMPORTANT MEDICAL UPDATE, it had read, so she had opened it automatically, imagining it would be some new, bad thing about her child.

But it wasn't about Leth at all.

The problem was with her. Not related to Leth's condition at all, just a run-of-the-mill human health problem. Her vision had never been perfect and there had been surgery twice before. But the results of her last test indicated that she needed intervention yet again. Her close vision, the message said, was deteriorating more quickly than they were comfortable with. She would need surgery again.

On Titan.

Panic ran through Evelyn like an electric current. It wasn't the surgery, the problem, the existential threat to herself. It was what she had to say to Leth now. Because the first time Leth was old enough to ask why only the two of them remained on Enceladus, she had lied and said that, while they were both okay, there was something in them that could possibly hurt others and they weren't going to take any risks.

It had been intended to reassure and it wasn't as if Evelyn was going to leave. And she did not feel guilt for the infection, no negative effects on Leth's physical health appeared. But there was guilt over the circumstances of her childhood. The isolation, the cold and dark. Before all this, Evelyn had imagined that one day she and Aerin and Leth would go to Earth and Leth could know directly the sound of wind and rain and birds.

Instead, what she had given her child could not have been more different than her own experience. No wonder Leth had always liked her stories.

"Zaza? What's the matter? You don't look well."

"No. I'm not," she said faintly.

"What?"

Taking a shuddering breath, she looked at her child.

"The results of my last physical. I am going to need an operation. Don't worry, it's not a dangerous thing, but I will have to go to Titan."

Leth's face was a mask of confusion. "What are you talking about, going to Titan? We're not allowed to do that."

"Leth," she said unsteadily. Pull that bandage off, she thought, and let the words tumble out. "We're not both quarantined here. You are. When the others left, it was because we had discovered you had experienced physical changes that connect you to Enceladus. None of the rest of us had those changes, but UNSpace didn't want to take any chances, so they were evacuated."

Evelyn couldn't look at Leth as she finished.

"It's just me?" Leth said. "We're here because of me."

And Evelyn watched her precious child stomp out of the room.

•　　　•　　　•

"I don't want to talk to you," Leth said over the person-to-person communications channel as Evelyn approached. Leth was leaning against the tool box beside the sensor array, looking south, a bike propped against the supply chest nearby.

Evelyn put her bike beside Leth's and walked over to the tool box, settling in beside her child, but not too close, willing to wait for the right moment.

"You lied to me," Leth eventually said, and turned to look directly at Evelyn. "Why couldn't you just tell me that it was something in me? Why would you say it was both of us? Why would you let me think that?"

"I didn't want you to feel like it was your fault," Evelyn said, her heart heavy with regret.

"But all this time I thought," Leth paused, as if to try and find the next words. "I thought you understood."

"What do you mean?" Evelyn asked with a twist to her stomach.

"Do you hear the dragons or not?" Leth said slowly.

"What?"

Flooding into Evelyn's mind were every mention of the dragons that Leth had ever made. Evelyn had always considered them an enchanting example of the broadness of childhood imagination.

"You don't, do you? When I told you about them, I thought you understood what I was saying." Leth began to pace back and forth in front of Evelyn. "I'm being literal when I tell you that they sing to me, in my mind. It depends on how strong the geysers are. Sometimes, I can hear them at the locus, but they're always clearer here."

"There is actually something for you to hear?" Evelyn stumbled over the words.

"Not hear, exactly. They are in my mind."

"What do they say?"

"It isn't words, it's more like feelings. Or ideas." Leth paused. "Concepts."

Evelyn had run out of words and could only stare at her child now.

"I thought you understood," Leth repeated.

●   ●   ●

Evelyn had packed her bag. She was sitting on the edge of her bed and staring at it. She wasn't sure what she was doing anymore.

The news of Leth's infection had been the single largest shift that she had ever had to incorporate. And she had spent the last seven years certain that nothing else would ever come close.

And yet here she was. In the course of a day, not even an entire Earth day, everything that she had thought she understood had changed.

Leth was both fine and not fine. Leth insisted that nothing was wrong, that there was happiness in the connection with Enceladus, with the dragons. That there was nothing negative or disturbing about it. At the same time, Leth had a hard time explaining the nature of the connection very clearly.

Grudgingly, Evelyn could accept that it was going to be difficult for a twelve year old who had lived with the situation for as long as they could remember to explain anything with clarity.

Her colleagues on Titan were merely excited by this new understanding of Leth's situation. Thrilled. Even Aerin. But they weren't here. They couldn't understand what she felt. The confusion, the worry.

UNSpace was now somewhat less concerned about Leth leaving, but when Evelyn suggested it to Leth, the response was quick and negative. In the end, they decided that Aerin would come to Enceladus while Evelyn was on Titan for an indeterminate length of time.

It was fine, of course, and Aerin was excited to come. But Evelyn had spent so long wanting her family to be together again, that this further, slight delay felt worse than it should have. If she was honest with herself, she wanted this part of their lives to be done, for Leth to be like she was before, and for all of them to go elsewhere.

But that wasn't going to happen any time soon.

"Zaza? The shuttle is about to land."

"Coming."

She joined Leth at the comms station and they watched on the large wall screen as the shuttle descended to the surface. Tentatively, she put her arm around Leth.

"I'm sorry I was wrong," she said.

"What do you mean?"

"I was wrong about everything. I've been unhappy here and I didn't want to blame you for that, so I assumed that you were unhappy, too. I was so focused on making sure you were physically okay that I ignored the things that you were saying to me."

Leth looked confused. "It's okay."

Evelyn nodded, knowing that she was even now doing a poor job of explaining herself. It was as if she were talking to herself.

Leth hugged her.

"I'm going to miss you, Zaza. You need to come back home as soon as you can."

Home.

A moment of stark realization crashed down on Evelyn, that when Leth recalled the summer days of childhood there would be no sound of wind and rain, no riding a bike down a bumpy dirt road.

It would be dark and cold, wrapped in a bulky spacesuit, traveling over ice on a bike that was large and solid, while the moon itself spoke to her.

It was not Evelyn's idea of perfection, but it would be Leth's.

Evelyn squeezed her child's shoulder.

"I'll be back as soon as I can."

WHAT IS A GIRL WITHOUT A DRAGON?

Gretchin Lair

C aitlin was collecting bits of melted glass and metal when she saw a flash of red and gold in the darkest corner of the garage. It was the only part of this house still intact after the wildfires had swept through a few months ago.

She probably wasn't supposed to be here. But when she wasn't at school she tried to spend most of her time away from her new family. As long as she was back for dinner, the Powells didn't seem to mind.

Burnt boards and glass crunched beneath her feet, like bones and jewels in a dragon's lair. Above her, the ribs of the house remained, blackened at the edges. The smell of smoke and tar still hung in the air. The darkness deepened as she entered the garage, shrouding the objects inside: boxes and washing machines, car parts and mattress springs, tools and shelves.

The colors were dim, but the bright red of a sturdy mountain bike stood out. It was tucked in the corner, awkward and graceless, with garish gold writing splashed on its side: Dragon. Straight black handles stuck out like wings. Its big tires were as knobbled as scales. Its frame was scratched and scuffed, its top bar oddly kinked. The ragged edges of the gear cluster narrowed into an inscrutable iris. The dust Caitlin disturbed as she shuffled closer twisted like smoke in a shaft of light, and she watched as it curled around the bike.

She heard a sound then, deep and breathy, something between a growl and a sigh. Caitlin paused, heart pounding. She didn't feel scared, just cautious.

Caitlin's pockets were still filled with the treasures she had gathered from the other burnt houses. She knew dragons liked treasure. Maybe Dragon had lost its hoard in the fire. Maybe she could win its favor. She had experience placating powerful, dangerous creatures. A dragon wasn't nearly as scary as her mom.

Carefully, she dug through her pockets and placed two tarnished coins in front of Dragon.

Another low sound, like a purr. She could feel it in her sneakers. Dragon was pleased at her offering. Caitlin smiled a little, but then looked at her watch and sighed. It was late. She turned to go, but Dragon stopped her with a huff.

"What?" she said, her voice loud in the silence. "I can't take you with me."

Dragon said nothing.

"What would I tell Mary and Dave?"

Dragon said nothing, but she knew it wanted to leave this place. It had been trapped here a long time, waiting, alone. Lonely. There was nothing for it here.

"They're not going to believe me. Grown-ups never believe you." Any time Caitlin had told the truth she had been punished for it. But Dragon clearly wanted to be rescued. It needed out. It needed a friend.

"Fine," she sighed. "But you'll need to hide until I figure out a good story, okay?"

Dragon was a big bike, too big for a 9-year-old girl, but she clumsily wrestled it out of the garage. The tires were low, but still rideable.

Dragon ticked and clattered as they rode slowly around the deserted cul-de-sac, chain rattling against the frame. Caitlin steered in wide and wavering circles, Dragon flexing its wings until they finally gained enough momentum to leave the scorched and hollowed homes behind.

·   ·   ·

She got back just in time. Caitlin still wasn't used to all the commotion at meal times, the clattering and bustling that happened when four kids, two adults, two dogs, two cats, and the chickens all needed to be fed at the same time. The plates rattled, the pressure cooker hissed, the dogs barked. Daniel liked to blow milk through his nose just to make everyone laugh. She hadn't known families could be like that. Caitlin's dinners had always been by herself in the kitchen, chewing corn chips and bologna sandwiches as quietly as possible so her mom wouldn't hear her from the living room where she watched TV. Caitlin loved meals with this family now, but sometimes it was overwhelming.

Mary spotted her first.

"Caitlin! I was wondering where you were!" she said with a broad smile, making a salad.

The other kids were already here: Daniel was feeding the dogs, even though the dogs were making it difficult, trying to eat directly from the bag. Todd was setting the table, and Jenna lifted her book as he set a plate in front of her.

Daniel ran up to Caitlin in his clumsy way, leaving the bag for the dogs.

"Hey, Caitlin! What comes down but never goes up?" He slurred his words, but his enthusiasm was sweet.

"I don't know, Daniel," she said. "What?" He was always asking her riddles, and didn't care that she never guessed.

"Rain," Jenna said, not turning around.

"RAIN!" Daniel shouted, smiling his biggest smile, the one that showed the hole in the roof of his mouth.

Mary's husband, Dave, came in from feeding the chickens. He shooed the dogs away from the bag and put it away.

"Hey, whose bike is that outside?" he said, pulling off his flannel jacket. Everyone turned towards him except Jenna, who turned a page.

"Uh," Caitlin said. She thought she would have more time to think of an excuse. "Dr. Hartwell gave it to me. She said it would be good for me." Caitlin was pretty sure this was a good lie. Nobody questioned Dr. Hartwell when she made a request, whether it was for appointments or supplies. "She got it from a toy drive, I think?" Caitlin improvised, suddenly interested in washing her hands.

As she turned, she crashed into Todd, who was carrying silverware. Forks fell from his hands. Todd was the oldest of the kids, about to graduate high school. But he was also Mary and Dave's actual son, so she had always been nervous around him. He seemed nice, but if she made him mad, she might get sent away.

"Oh, no, I'm sorry!" Caitlin froze, cringing. But nobody yelled at her, nobody grabbed her roughly, nobody kicked over a chair. Todd just bent to pick up the forks, while Dave grabbed more forks from the silverware drawer.

"It's okay, Caitlin," Dave murmured. "Go sit at the table."

She wished she had helped pick up the forks. That probably would have been a better thing to do than just stand there. Stupid Caitlin. But then she heard Dragon rumble from the porch. The sound was strange and comforting at the same time.

"Hey, Daniel," she said, scooting her chair forward. "I have a riddle for you! What is a dragon without a treasure to protect?"

Daniel was so happy to have a new riddle he didn't seem to care how strange it sounded. She didn't even know if she had an answer. But it was going to be fun to hear him guess.

•   •   •

"I'm going to have to thank Dr. Hartwell," Dave said as he detached the tire pump. "Todd hasn't had a bike in years, and we never thought about getting one for any of our foster kids."

Caitlin held her breath. She hoped he would forget. Grown-ups often said things they forgot about later.

Dave pushed Dragon towards her. He had wiped it down and checked the brakes.

"After school it should be a straight shot to your appointment. Be careful, okay?"

Caitlin nodded and tried to look confident. Her mom had given her a bike for Christmas, but had taken it away a few weeks later when Caitlin was bad. Caitlin always seemed to be bad. No matter how hard she tried to do everything her mom said, she was always wrong.

As soon as she grasped Dragon's handlebars, she felt Dragon surge forward, clearly straining to reach the street. Dave followed her to wave from the driveway.

And then she was off, trying hard not to wobble. With freshly inflated tires, she could hear Dragon's deep purr clearly as they rolled along the road, and with each passing moment, her grin widened. She felt like she was flying. She felt like she was free.

After school she biked to Dr. Hartwell, the case manager she had to see every week. Caitlin loved how she and Dragon moved together through the streets and sidewalks. Dragon was bold but alert. Nothing had ever made Caitlyn feel more invincible.

Enough of a smile remained on Caitlin's face that Dr. Hartwell commented on it when she entered the room: "Hello, Caitlin! You must be having a good day!"

Caitlin never knew how to act around Dr. Hartwell. She seemed friendly enough, and always asked Caitlin about her feelings, but Caitlin didn't know what was safe to tell her. What if her mom found out? Caitlin's smile vanished. Dragon, waiting outside, crouched cautiously.

Dr. Hartwell motioned for Caitlin to sit.

"I have some big news for you today!"

Caitlin held her face still. "Big news" was never good news, no matter how much grown-ups wanted you to believe it was.

"Your dad's decided to sue for custody. That means you'll be living with the Powells for a little longer while the case gets decided."

Caitlin watched Dr. Hartwell's lips move as she kept speaking, but Caitlin's ears rang as Dragon roared in surprise and shock. Flames rose inside her, smoke filling her lungs, making it hard to breathe.

Caitlin's mom used to complain bitterly about her dad and his girlfriend Diane ("that homewrecking bitch"). Caitlin only saw them for a couple of weeks each summer, but she thought Diane was nice. They played games together. Diane watched Caitlin practice roller-skating in the driveway.

She even made her a German chocolate cake for her birthday and said, "Make a wish!" as Caitlin blew out the candles.

But Caitlin didn't remember much of her dad from those visits. He was tall, with a bushy mustache and long hair. He joked a lot and always had a beer in his hand. But what she mostly remembered about her dad was that he didn't seem to notice whether she was there or not. Why did he want her now?

"Caitlin?"

She blinked, the roar of the flames fading.

"You have an important job," Dr. Hartwell repeated. "We want you to tell us who you'd rather live with: your mom, or your dad? We want what's best for you, so we can't guarantee that's where you'll go, but we'll be sure to take that into consideration."

Now Caitlin was cold. Dragon climbed high into the atmosphere, where the air was thin and sharp, before plummeting to the ground as if snared by a heavy chain.

"Can't I just stay where I am?"

Dr. Hartwell frowned with a complex expression that reminded Caitlin of Diane. "I'm sorry, no, that's not an option."

Caitlin didn't want to live with her mom. But Dr. Hartwell said she couldn't guarantee anything. What if Caitlin chose her dad, and they decided to make her live with her mom anyway? Dragon writhed as it tried to escape the trap.

"They're both nice . . ." Caitlin lied. Dragon's tail thrashed like an agitated cat's. Caitlin picked up one of Dr. Hartwell's pretty pens, clicking it nervously.

Dr. Hartwell tilted her head. "If your mom agrees to an anger-management class and a parenting support group, the court will probably rule in her favor. Is that what you want?"

Oh. Caitlin's mom was good at acting. She could fool the court. That made it even more important that she never find out Caitlin didn't want to be with her.

Dragon moaned with resignation and frustration: a dark, harrowing sound. "I don't care," Caitlin mumbled, surreptitiously slipping the pen into her pocket.

"Right," Dr. Hartwell said, dubiously. "Well, take some time to think about it. We'll talk about this again next week."

•   •   •

The decision weighed on Caitlin's shoulders like a heavy cloak every time she visited Dr. Hartwell. But no matter how Dr. Hartwell asked, Caitlin always said the same thing: "I don't care."

Other than those weekly meetings, the next few months were the best Caitlin had ever had. Summer finally came, with free time and long days. Her mom hated summer and used to keep the house dark, staying in her bedroom with a wet washcloth as Caitlin tried to keep quiet. This summer every ride with Dragon was a quest, exploring new lands. Mary and Dave even let her take Dragon to the convenience store to pick up milk.

Caitlin's favorite place was at the top of a trail so steep she had to dismount Dragon to climb it. They would walk together the rest of the way to sit beneath a wide oak tree overlooking the river. Her legs swung over the side of the cliff as she watched clouds as bright as china plates against the blue sky. Dragon would lean against the tree and close its eyes, or listen to her sing. She would never dream of singing in front of anyone else, but Dragon told her she had a nice voice.

Dragon wanted a hoard, so they gathered treasures like glass, foil, beads, stones, feathers, coins, bottle caps, keys, and paper clips she sometimes took from Dr. Hartwell. She loved when she found something she knew Dragon would covet, like a marble half-buried in the ground. Lost jewelry was the best: earrings and bracelets and rings with precious stones, even if they were plastic. Once, Dragon wanted a tiny purple flashlight from the convenience store, so she took it. Dragon was delighted.

But being at the house with everyone was nice, too. Todd was learning magic and was pleased to have an audience. Daniel kept trying to find a riddle Jenna didn't know the answer to. Caitlin was now responsible for feeding the chickens and gathering eggs. She was beginning to think of this place as home.

One day, Jenna came into the room they shared and unceremoniously thrust something at Caitlin.

"Here," Jenna said. Caitlin wasn't surprised to see it was a book. Jenna went to the library every Tuesday after visiting her grandma in the hospital. Nobody knew what would happen to Jenna when her grandma died. That's why she was staying with Mary and Dave. Her sisters were with another foster family.

Caitlin took the book from Jenna. On the cover was a huge red dragon, letters stamped in gold across its body: *THE COMPLETE DRAGON*. Dragon twitched in anticipation.

"Thanks, Jenna," she said, surprised and touched. This was the first time Jenna had lent her a book. Or anything, for that matter. Jenna usually kept to herself, only occasionally complaining about Caitlin's messy collections of water glasses and food wrappers.

"I like dragons," Jenna declared. "Dragons are smart." Jenna's hair fell in front of her face. It was mousy and thin, like she was. It was easy to forget Jenna was younger than Caitlin because she was so serious all the time and read so much.

"Yeah," Caitlin said. "I guess." Of course Dragon was smart, but she wasn't sure if all dragons were.

"No, really!" Jenna said. "Like, they know all the languages and never get lost and they like riddles! And they know magic! And everyone thinks they're mean but they are actually really loyal. Like your dragon!"

"It's not my dragon," Caitlin said. "It's just Dragon."

"Oh," Jenna said. Then: "Does it have a name?"

"No," Caitlin said. "It's just Dragon."

"Is it a boy dragon or a girl dragon?"

Caitlin shook her head, a little annoyed. "It's just Dragon!" If she had been talking to Daniel, she would have put it in the form of a riddle: What is a dragon if it's not a boy or a girl?

"Hmmm," Jenna said, clearly not satisfied. "Well, anyway, you can tell Dragon I really like it. And I can give it a name when it wants one. It should have a really good name!"

This was probably the longest conversation Caitlin had ever had with Jenna. Dragon preened like a peacock, its scales glittering like embers.

Jenna picked up another book from one of her many piles. "I'm going to give this one to Daniel," she said, taking a book of riddles with her as she left.

· · ·

Fear and fury whipped through Caitlin like wildfire after her mom's supervised visit at Dr. Hartwell's office. Caitlin hadn't seen her mom since Caitlin had been taken away. She hated her mom's sickly sweet voice, as bright as ice, acting as if nothing had happened. Caitlin knew her mom wouldn't try anything as long as Dr. Hartwell was watching, but she could see an Evil Queen squirming beneath her mom's nicey-nice mask and cringed when the Queen tried to hug her.

Caitlin couldn't escape fast enough. Caitlin and Dragon flew through the streets until they took a corner too quickly and Dragon slipped beneath them. They fell as suddenly and sharply as if slain by a sword.

Now Dragon lay between the curb and the street, glaring at her in the sun. But why was Dragon mad at her? If she got sent back to her mom, Caitlin knew she couldn't protect Dragon. But shouldn't Dragon have protected *her* today?

Caitlin's tears quenched the flames, transforming anger into hurt. Her blood pounded in her ears. Her scrapes stung as if singed. She expected Dragon to apologize or to comfort her. But it didn't. The silence between them was deafening.

Finally, Caitlin walked Dragon back home. She dropped it in the yard, letting it fall in the dirt, then limped into the house, still smoldering.

As she opened the door, she almost bumped into Todd carrying a big box to the car. She had forgotten Todd was leaving in the morning for college, even though there had been boxes around for weeks.

"Sorry," she said automatically.

"What happened to you?" Todd said.

"Nothing," Caitlin said, trying to slide by.

"You're hurt," Todd said, putting the box down. "Come on, let's get some Band-Aids."

Todd took her to the master bathroom in Mary and Dave's room, a place she had never been. He carefully washed her scrapes, smoothed ointment on them to soothe the burning, then covered them with bandages.

He smiled at her. "How's that?"

"Better," Caitlin said. "Thanks."

"You want to see a magic trick?" Todd asked as he pulled a coin from behind her ear. Caitlin flinched. Dragon would have loved that trick, but she didn't want to think about Dragon right now.

"Show me something else," she said. Her eyes widened with an idea. "Show me how to do fire!"

Todd shook his head and made a face. "My parents would kill me if I did that. They're still spooked from the big fire last year."

"Your parents wouldn't kill you!" Caitlin said, genuinely surprised. "Your parents are great! I wish they were my parents."

Todd's lips twisted. "That's what everyone says. Everyone tells me how lucky I am. *Especially* my parents. I'm lucky that I have a good home, food to eat, parents who love me. Everyone tells me how my mom and dad are so generous and awesome and—sometimes I wish they weren't."

Caitlin's mouth gaped. "Why?"

Todd sighed. "I don't know. It's just . . . They expect me to be as perfect as they are. I have to take care of everybody, especially Daniel. But I didn't get a choice." Todd shrugged. "That's why I have to leave. It's not that I don't love them! I've just been waiting a long time to make my own decisions."

Caitlin didn't know what to say.

"So when are *you* leaving?" Todd asked, clearly changing the subject. "Aren't you supposed to decide between your mom and dad?"

"I don't care," Caitlin said, looking down.

Todd sighed and sat back. "Yeah, you do. But it's not a real choice. I get that. You got dealt a bad hand."

He spread his hands wide, a pack of Bicycle playing cards suddenly fanned in a perfect semicircle in front of her.

"Here, pick one," he said.

Caitlin stretched her hand out, trying to feel which card was the right one. Her hand wavered between cards before finally settling on one just to the left of center. She slid it out and turned it towards her.

"Good choice," Todd said, without even looking. "King of Diamonds."

Caitlin was relieved it wasn't a Queen. She smiled at Todd, eyes wide with wonder. "Wow! Teach me *that* trick!"

Todd grinned at her enthusiasm. "A magician never reveals his secrets! But that's what I love about magic. I mean, you know it's a trick, right? You know it's not real. But it's still magic! It's still *true*."

Caitlin nodded, thinking about Dragon. She tried to hand the card back.

"Keep it," Todd said. "Sometimes you don't get to choose the deck, but you *can* choose how you play the card." As he spoke, the deck disappeared, and he left the bathroom with a little flourish.

Caitlin bent her knee experimentally before following Todd. She felt a lot better. As she left, she saw a bowl of Mary's jewelry on the counter. A gold bracelet with bright red gems caught her eye. After a moment, she stuffed it and the card into her pocket.

When she got back to the yard, she saw Dragon flipped upside down in a patch of grass. Jenna was kneeling next to it. Was Jenna . . . rubbing Dragon's belly? The dogs loved that, but Caitlin didn't know dragons liked it, too.

"What are you doing?" Caitlin said, her flames fully forgotten.

"The derailleur is bent," Jenna said without turning around. "I think we can just bend it back. None of the spokes are broken, though, and the frame still looks OK."

Caitlin stared at her in amazement. "How . . . do you know all that?"

Jenna turned around. She had messily braided her hair to keep it out of her way. "I got a bunch of bike books at the library. Duh."

Caitlin smiled. "OK, thanks. I should probably let Dave look at it."

"We can fix it!" Jenna insisted. "I mean, he knows how to pump up the tires, but *anyone* can do that!"

"Have you even ridden a bike before?"

"No," Jenna said, defensively. "But I've read about it. I can figure it out."

Caitlin laughed. "It's not the same thing! You can't learn how to ride a bike from reading a book!"

"Oh, yeah?" Jenna said. She grabbed Dragon and flipped it back over with surprising ease for her small size. Caitlin always struggled with Dragon when she moved it around, but it was like Jenna knew just where to place her hands to balance its weight. Caitlin was about to ask Jenna about it when she realized Jenna was actually trying to mount Dragon.

Caitlin grabbed Dragon's handlebars. "Whoa, wait!"

"I can do it!" Jenna said, trying and failing to swing her leg over the seat.

"OK, OK, but wait, no," Caitlin said. If she didn't help, Jenna was going to hurt herself. "It's easier if you try to put your leg over this part here. See? It's a little lower."

Jenna adjusted her stance and managed to get one leg over the top bar. She was now astride Dragon. The bike was definitely too big for her, but Jenna clutched the handlebars fiercely.

"Now put your foot on the top pedal," Caitlin said. Jenna put up her left foot and the pedal swung backwards.

"Uh, no. Put your other foot up but don't push back. OK," Caitlin said, scrambling to figure out how to describe what Jenna should do. "Um, it's kinda complicated, but now you have to sort of push the pedal down, uh, forward, while you're trying to get up on the seat. Got it?"

Caitlin kept the bike steady as Jenna tried to fling herself forward and upward and backward all at the same time, pressing her lips together in concentration, trying to catch herself before bashing against the crossbar. On the sixth try, they were both surprised when Jenna successfully perched on the seat.

Jenna broke out into a huge grin. "See? I told you I could do it!"

Caitlin laughed. "Well, that's just the first step, right? Now you have to actually ride it."

But Caitlin wasn't able to balance both Dragon and Jenna while they were all moving. After almost falling a few times, Jenna awkwardly dismounted.

"Sorry," Caitlin said. "Dave or Mary could probably teach you better. But I guess if you want to learn, you can use this bike." *When I'm gone,* Caitlin didn't say.

Jenna's eyes were shining. "I can borrow Dragon?"

Caitlin felt a chill. She tried to smile. "Sure."

·   ·   ·

A few days later, Caitlin dropped her backpack in the sunroom. "Hello?" she called. The house was quieter than she had ever heard. Her neck prickled. Where was everyone? She couldn't even hear the dogs or the chickens. Dragon was quiet, but alert.

"I'm in here, Caitlin," Mary's voice called from the kitchen. There was something flat about her tone. Caitlin almost choked on the surge of fear that rose into her throat. The light seemed dim, sooty.

If she could have hidden in her bedroom without going through the kitchen, she would have. Instead, she slunk into the kitchen, keeping away from Mary, who was sitting at the table.

"Hi, Caitlin," she said. Instead of the energetic smile she usually had, her face was composed and solemn. Her voice was still warm, but worn.

"Hi," Caitlin said, giving Mary a wide berth.

"Caitlin, we need to talk," Mary said.

Caitlin cringed. So this was it. After the supervised visit, Caitlin knew it was only a matter of time before they sent her back to her mom. She longed to escape on Dragon again, but she couldn't let Dragon be captured by the Queen.

Mary's tone softened. "Don't worry, Caitlin. I'm not going to hurt you. Sit down."

Caitlin pulled out a chair, her mouth dry.

"I want you to tell me the truth, okay?"

Caitlin's mom used to say that: "Just tell me the truth." But her mom never meant it. Did Mary? Caitlin nodded. Nodding was almost always the right answer at this point.

Mary paused. Then, mildly: "Where did the bike really come from?"

Caitlin's face flushed as hot and red as Dragon. "I told you," she said, her voice quavering.

"We talked to Dr. Hartwell," Mary said. "She was worried when you ran out after your mom's visit. She had no idea what we were talking about when we tried to thank her for the bike."

Caitlin couldn't speak. Her mouth opened and closed uselessly. Her eyes filled with hot tears.

Mary waited for her to speak. Finally, Caitlin said, "It was at one of the burned houses out by the ridge."

Mary looked at her, evaluating. "Why didn't you tell us the truth to begin with?" she asked. Her voice was still mild.

"You wouldn't have believed me," Caitlin mumbled. "You wouldn't have let me keep it."

"Oh, Caitlin," Mary sighed. "We've been foster parents for a long time now. We've seen everything. You can trust us. But how can we trust you if you don't tell us the truth?"

Caitlin felt wounded, as if an arrow had pierced the soft spot beneath her scales. Her tears spilled over, scalding her cheeks. Mary reached forward. "It's okay, Caitlin!"

"No!" Caitlin shrugged Mary's arms aside. Everyone had been so nice to her here. How could she be trusted if she didn't tell the truth? A dragon never apologized, but a dragon was not a girl.

"I . . . I took your bracelet. I'm sorry! I'm sorry!" Caitlin's mom used to make her say 'sorry' a lot, even though Caitlin wasn't always sure why she was saying it. It was a magic word that sometimes worked to calm her mom when she was mad. But now Caitlin felt what it should have meant all along.

Mary's expression melted into disappointment. Caitlin ran towards her bedroom, sobbing. One of the cats jumped off Jenna's bed, alarmed, skittering through the door just before Caitlin closed it.

Caitlin heard Mary's phone ring, giving her a few moments to cry alone. She couldn't make out any words, but Mary's tone was soothing. Slowly, Caitlin's pounding heart slowed, her sniffles dwindled. She wiped the tears that had leaked from her eyes to her ears.

A few minutes later, Mary knocked on the door and entered. Caitlin turned over in bed, facing away from her. Mary sat on the edge of Caitlin's bed and waited, her hand on Caitlin's back.

Finally, Caitlin said, "Are you going to kick me out now?"

"No," Mary said. "We'd never kick you out. But," Mary paused. "Dr. Hartwell called again. She says the court decided to give your dad custody. He'll be here next week."

Caitlin sat up. "What?! But my mom! The visit!"

Mary looked surprised. "Oh, honey! Have you been worried about that this whole time? That was just a supervised visit. That's part of what went into the judgment. It didn't mean you were going to go back."

Caitlin fell back against the bed. "But why can't I just stay with you?" she said, her voice strained.

"Oh, honey, no. That's not how this works. Everyone leaves. Well, Daniel might not leave, but he still needs us. We're only here for as long as you need us. Why don't you want to go with your dad?"

"He doesn't care if I'm there or not."

"Why didn't you choose your mom, then?"

Caitlin stiffened. Her voice cracked as she said, "I can't go back to her. I can't."

Mary rubbed her arm. "I know. You don't have to go back. It's scary to go with your dad because you haven't seen him in a long time. But I've seen you change a lot since you've been here. You've been very brave. It might not be perfect, but it's definitely going to be better than living with your mom. Trust me."

Caitlin slowly relaxed. Now that the decision had been made, Caitlin wished she had been brave enough to make it. And now she could probably take Dragon with her. She wanted Dragon to meet Diane.

After a long silence, Mary's hands stilled.

"Where's the bracelet?" Mary asked, lightly.

Caitlin leaned over the side of the bed to find the shoebox with Dragon's hoard. Her head pounded as she sifted through it until she snagged the sparkling bracelet. She rolled over and handed it to Mary.

"Thank you," Mary said. "Tashonna gave me this bracelet before she left a couple of years ago. She said she wanted to leave something behind so I wouldn't forget her. It's very special to me." She paused. "But I might have let you borrow it if you had asked."

One of the cats meowed and scratched outside the door. Mary let the cat in as she left the room, and Caitlin felt it jump lightly onto the bed, kneading and turning until finally settling beside her. Then Dragon wrapped around her, gently rumbling as she drifted to sleep.

•   •   •

Caitlin's heart hammered as a blue car pulled into the Powells's driveway. She remembered this feeling from the wildfires last year, when the air was thick and everyone was afraid. But it had been beautiful, too, with a copper sun and white ash staining her shirt with afternoon stars. Now the grass was growing back, tender shoots pushing through the blackened ground.

The dogs began barking immediately. Dave was already walking down the steps, while Mary stayed on the porch with her arms loosely wrapped around Daniel, who wiggled excitedly. Caitlin rolled a deep ruby marble between her fingers as she waited, the only piece of Dragon's treasure she had decided to keep. Todd's card was safely in her pocket.

She wished Jenna was here, too, but Jenna had refused to say goodbye. "Leave me alone! I'm reading!" she shouted from behind their bedroom door.

When she had originally asked Jenna to help her prepare Dragon for its journey, Caitlin saw Jenna's face close like a book. For the rest of the week Jenna avoided everyone, staying in her room or at the library whenever possible. She wouldn't even answer Daniel's riddles. Dragon had first fumed, then fretted, then became forlorn before Caitlin finally understood:

Dragon needed to stay. It was connected to Jenna by fine golden chains Caitlin never knew were there.

So today Caitlin had planned to bring Jenna out on the porch for a ceremony as solemn as a knighting, leaving Dragon in Jenna's care. She would have spoken of Dragon's loyalty and Jenna's intelligence, asking them both to commit to the virtues of valor and adventure. Then she would have tapped Jenna on each shoulder with a ruler while telling them to take care of each other. She had imagined Jenna's rarest smile and Dragon's satisfaction warming her as she drove away, as perfect as any fairy tale ending.

Now Caitlin was heartbroken she wouldn't have the chance to wrap everything up as neatly and cleverly as she had hoped. But Dragon understood. Dragon was patient. With time running out, Caitlin wrote a note and tucked it inside one of Jenna's library books:

Dragon wants to stay with you. I know you will take good care of it. Please give it a good name!

In the remaining space, she had scribbled a riddle Daniel had told her:

P.S.: Why do dragons sleep all day? They like to hunt Knights!

It didn't feel like enough, but it was all she could do before she had to leave. For now, Dragon leaned against the house, a bike instead of a dragon.

Caitlin could only see shadows moving in the car. She was burning with curiosity and flooded with dread at the same time. But then the doors opened, and when she saw who was getting out of the passenger side, a spark flared in Caitlin's chest.

"Hi, Diane!" she yelled, running forward.

THE MOTHERS OF PEQUEÑO LAGO

Kate Macdonald

Elena braked, and stopped with a wet slide of tires in front of the twisted tree branch projecting across the ditch.

"Breathe. Don't move," she told herself, crouched over her handlebars. She kept one leg braced on the road.

The rain continued to pour. Then there was movement. The vast claws clutching the road surface, four metres in front of her, dragged through the tarmac like knives through marzipan. She could see by the dragon's glow that her hind leg had braced to take her weight. Something was about to happen.

·   ·   ·

The two dragons had entered Spanish air space over Asturias early in June, shimmering in the heat. Flashes of light reflected from their scales as they glided and soared over the mountain ranges. A national park warden looked back nervously from the file of evacuating campers that she was urging down the trail.

"They're searching for something. Keep moving!"

The larger dragon was circling indolently, but with purpose, and the other followed her at a distance.

In a day, the female dragon had established her mating arena on a spike-ridged plateau in the Picos. It was above a broad-bottomed valley used by a stock cartel as a nursery for the bull-rings. The smaller, nimbler male dragon hooked the bulls up into the air by their long white horns during his showy courtship flights. He tossed them to the female, or simply charred them in the air. Their bones littered the valley floor. When the bulls had all been eaten, the dragons scooped up sheep from the neighbouring valley. The local ibex had long since moved southward to safer territories.

The dragons' mating flight was spectacular, lasting from midday until well into the night with fireballs and roaring. Foolhardy spectators peered cautiously at the soaring beasts from behind rocky outcrops on neighbouring peaks, and helicopters ran flights for television crews. The dragons ignored observers who took care to stay still, but the helicopter flights were stopped when four passengers from Madrid and their pilot were incinerated in mid-air. Camera drones were also not tolerated.

After the mating act had been achieved, explosively, with deafening roars, the dragons settled on the southern edge of their mountain. They draped themselves over the rocky ridges to bask in the sun, and sent jets of fire at traffic going to and from the lake below. The road was closed abruptly. The villagers of Pequeño Lago, at the end of the abandoned road, were instructed by the government to hike out of their valley at night through the surrounding forest. Most managed to leave the valley in a week, but then the dragons tore through the forest while hunting, and its resinous pine trees burned briskly for days. The air force stood down from its planned operation. The remaining villagers were trapped, hunkered down on rationed food to await the dragons' pleasure.

When it became known that two heavily pregnant women were among the village hostages, media hysteria escalated. Stories and photographs of the impending mothers of Pequeño Lago became the news. Maria Fano Rochas was already a mother of three, but the unmarried Carmen Barrio Martinez was due to give birth to her first child by the end of July. She spoke to her best friend Elena Cascos Fernández, a student midwife at the hospital in Llanes, almost every evening by phone. They joked, they laughed, they discussed recipes for the dwindling food. Carmen had cravings for fresh eggs, but the chickens had gone. Elena ignored her own anxiety and rallied her friend with episodes of a soap opera they created from her ward sister's passion for the catering head.

"She goes looking for him every time she comes off shift. She demanded that he meet her in the evenings, but he's married. His wife works in osteopathy, and she is seriously scary. Built like a wrestler."

"Which one has access to scalpels?" Carmen interrupted.

"Both, but he's got kitchen knives!"

Carmen cackled, but her heart wasn't in it. 'Did you see on the news what those dragons have done to our vineyard? If we survive this, it'll take years to restock, and rebuild.'

Elena said stoutly "You'll survive. Just hang on, keep your head down. What's the baby doing now?"

"Headbutting me. She's been doing it for hours."

"Go to sleep. I'll be here, but go to sleep."

The male dragon departed without ceremony towards the end of June. The big female remained reclining on the mountain ridge, and permitted vultures to scavenge among the discarded remnants of her meals. Over the next four weeks, military observations determined that her belly was increasingly distended, and her glowing scales had settled in color to a greenish gold. Zoologists debated the gestation period of dragons, and classicists and palaeoarchaeologists were consulted to consider clutch size. Never before had a dragon awaited the laying of her eggs so publicly.

The crisis began when Maria's fourth child made her entrance into the world five weeks early. Her Llanes gynecologist directed proceedings remotely via Skype to Maria's husband and her mother-in-law, and all went well. But this trial run of a home birth without medical attendants made it grimly clear how little equipment the village had, and how dangerous the birth could be for Carmen, already suffering a little from hypertension. The Spanish air force attempted a stealth drop of instruments and medication, but the dragon put her foot down: the drone and its packages were crushed into the muddy edges of the lake when she went to drink.

The hospital and the media demanded action to save the mothers and babies of Pequeño Lago. Poisoned bait had been tried, but the artfully placed carcasses had been ignored, since dragons do not eat carrion. The air force admitted that while their sophisticated precision-targeted weaponry was ready to inflict a direct, eliminating strike, Pequeño Lago would probably also be destroyed, since—if blasted out of the sky—the dragon was highly likely to fall onto the village. The beast would have to be attacked in flight over the mountains, but even that was risky. Who knew where her body would land? Or what she would do if the missiles went awry? The zoologists advised waiting for the eggs to be laid, after which the dragon would rise to hunt, and might be attacked over a less populated region.

When Carmen's waters broke, Elena was on placement in a large village sixteen kilometres up the valley from Pequeño Lago. It was a moonless night, and the new baby whose birth she and her supervisor Dolores had been attending was sound asleep. They were packing their instruments when Carmen WhatsApped Elena in a panic.

"OK, don't worry about the mess. Get into something dry and warm, and if the contractions begin, time them. Dolores is here, she's going to call you back. Keep talking to her, tell her everything that's happening. She's the best midwife we have, you'll be fine. I'll see you soon: I'm coming to help."

Elena ran back to her room in the nurses dormitory. She repacked her midwife's bag, muffling her instruments with sterile dressing packs.

"Syringes, gauze, gloves, postnatal pads, sterile water tubes," she muttered, strapping the bag. "Scissors, forceps, sutures, needles, thermometer, chocolate." She squeezed the bag into her largest backpack, and shoved her fleece jacket on top. She ran down the stairs and outside to the bike shed.

Her bike hubs and chain were already oiled, the bearings had been repacked a week ago, and the brakes were newly serviced. She turned off her phone, freewheeled without lights down the hill, and rode silently out of the village. It was one forty-five in the morning, and no one was around. She took the south fork towards the lake, and sped downhill on the road to Pequeño Lago. Her heart was no longer thumping. The cold panic in her stomach had settled, though there were too many uncertainties ahead. What if the dragon smelt her?

"I can do it," she thought grimly. "I'll save Carmen and her baby if I die trying."

Elena eased left into the first turn and again to the right, taking the first switchback gently, not daring to risk the sound of wheels on the road's gravel edge.

She'd just delivered a baby in a rapid birth, and Maria's mother-in-law was still in the village to help. She would not think of risks, she would do her job, and bring that baby out safely. And get past the dragon. Holy Mother of God, she had to get past the dragon.

She heard an owl hunting for food, and wondered if the dragon had left it anything to eat. She could feel cool air rushing through the vents in her helmet, but she was certain she was making no noise. The urgency, and the terror ahead of getting past the dragon, had gone. Elena knew that this was the best ride she'd ever taken. Exultation started to flood her senses, but she clamped it down.

"Don't be cocky," she muttered. "You can't fool a dragon." She didn't feel despair, as she ought to, so close to a dragon's lair, but she knew she was cold with fear.

Elena sped on, managing twists and turns with judicious braking, uncertain what the dragons might have done to the road's surface. The dragon's phosphorescence glowed like a miasma in the night, making the hillside above the lake a jagged patch of shadows. At seven kilometres down, two burnt-out cars lay on their sides. The broken carcass of a dog lay half in the ditch, half out. Two turns in the road later, an abandoned van with its doors open blocked the outer lane, on the cliff edge. Rain began to fall, heavily, splashing noisily on her helmet and hands. She glanced up at the sky and saw the dragon's glow on the low cloud above her. She cycled on, freewheeling and braking in turn, nursing her bike in a silent, dogged run downhill.

Then she met the claws in the road, and smelled an acrid metallic discharge from the dragon's skin. She exhaled silently, almost wobbling with relief, thinking, "Thank God. That'll mask my scent."

The dragon's tail was raised, and she was straddling the valley with her pendulous belly hanging low over the lake. One hind leg was gouging the scorched vineyards to the south while the other gripped the road, the forelegs lost somewhere in the higher valley ground to the east. She made periodic yowling roars, and gripped the road and the earth ferociously.

Elena crouched, watching, at the side of the road, her backpack safe on her back, and her bike lying silently on its side.

Before the dawn came, Elena had observed her first dragon accouchement. The dragon's glow illuminated the pulses rippling down her taut abdomen, and she generated enough heat to dry Elena's sweating face with blasts of labouring air. Elena did not see the first egg drop into the darkness below the road edge, but she heard the dragon's outbreath of hiss. The metallic stink thickened, and Elena ducked her chin into her scarf, pulling it over her nose. There was a heavy thud as the egg was received by the soft mud at the edge of the lake. More eggs followed, dropping into a pile of white globes that also glowed in the night. If she could lean forward, just a little, Elena would be able to see the scaly markings on the shells that would harden soon into armour. But she stayed crouched in the roadside ditch. The dragon hauled herself around and her hind claws gouged out more tarmac. She nosed at her clutch, but seemed restless. She was pushing at the eggs with her head, inexpertly, then looking around, searching for something. Elena did not move.

Extending her forelimb, the dragon scraped at the field edge and dragged earth and mud downward to pile around the eggs. They were not yet covered, and glowed like a fungus. The dragon shifted her weight, and grabbed with her other gigantic forelimb at the cliff and road edge to pull it downwards. Elena's bike slid down into the rockfall, and Elena fell with it. She hit stone with her shoulder and then landed in softer earth and scratchy weeds, her backpack covering her from sight. Covered in loose earth, bleeding, and her face running with tears, she was shielded from the dragon's direct view by a burned-out tree. Her bicycle was half-buried, its back wheel spinning madly, but the dragon ignored it. Elena wept in shock, wanting to scream aloud with the adrenaline surge, but clamped it down. She shook uncontrollably, and bit her lips and clenched her fists to stay still, keep silent, don't make a sound.

The dragon hauled herself away from the egg mound, and paused, sniffing at the air. There was a pause, and the hot rattling breathing of the delivered mother. Then without any warning she leapt, upwards into the sky with vast, whomphing flaps of her leathered wings. Elena crouched into a ball as loosened trees and stones tumbled past and around her, but nothing more hit her.

In the distance Elena saw the dragon fly higher into the western sky until her shape had fused into the dark blue of early dawn. The sound of her heaving wings was throbbing in Elena's ears, but she could also hear a tentative note of birdsong.

She pulled herself upright, shaking off the dirt and twigs, and put her hands against the egg mound before her, staring at the gently glowing eggs piled high. Their pallid surfaces seemed to move, or throb in the half-light. She stretched out a hand to touch the nearest shell, then pulled it back. The markings were getting darker, more distinct. She didn't have much time.

She twisted to tug her backpack off, and tore at the straps to get at her instrument bag. The egg shells would be hardening soon, and her job was helping babies to live. She found her box of latex gloves, and the instruments she needed, and pulled herself over the edge of the mound, down to the eggs.

After about an hour, when Elena had finished her work, dawn was well on its way. She saw the lights of an electric truck coming silently, cautiously down the road, and pulled herself out of the egg mound. When the truck doors opened to exclamations, and shouts, Elena was pulling the dripping gloves from her hands, next to the ruin of her bike. There were lights on in the village; she supposed she should be going there next. Two figures were running towards her. She walked forward unsteadily.

"I need new forceps. I broke mine on their heads," she said to them hoarsely, "They won't hatch now." She was crying, raging and exultant, and distraught, rubbing her hands convulsively down the sides of her filthy midwife's tunic. "I've been killing babies."

·   ·   ·

The dragons did not return to Asturias. They would, the animal psychologists explained, expect their brood to take the plateau for their own, and no dragon interferes in another's territory. The broken eggs were examined by zoologists, and their albumen provided the cell material for a new bacteriological deterrent for use on future dragon infestations.

Carmen's baby was a girl. She was named Draca.

BOOTLEG

Alice Pow

Candace teetered on the windowsill, looking out at the enormous factory room she was about to trespass into. Bots zoomed about with big cardboard boxes full of bike parts, handing them off to LoadBots which stacked them in the backs of trucks, which would deliver them to the houses with enough money to order one of these sets. The dim light barely illuminated her face, and she had to fight the urge to tremble as she balanced.

She thought about all the times she'd been commended in grade school for being well behaved. She hadn't gotten those sorts of comments since starting high school.

Directly below her was a conveyor belt where the packages entered the room. The bots all stayed on the opposite side, zipping back and forth to grab boxes. Candace watched, waiting for a lull around the belt, but the whole appeal of bots was that they did not lull. There was no need for motion tracking wristbands to jolt the idle hands of workers into alertness anymore.

Bots and machines did a lot of the human jobs now. Candace's mom used to drive trucks, but now trucks drove trucks. And sometimes Candace was happy because driving trucks is terribly risky, but more often she was also hungry and tired.

Candace's family was not an anomaly. Maia's parents used to own a bike store. She was the one who suggested Candace try biking after she quit soccer. The idea stuck, but neither of them knew where to get an affordable bike anymore.

She bit her lip and dropped down, pointing her left hand toward the ground and clicking the switch on the side of her index knuckle. A pulse of force escaped the device in her palm, cushioning her fall to the cold concrete floor. It was a PushPalm. Another Dragon.river, Inc. product she'd lifted.

As she landed, Candace stalled a moment, breathing slowly through her nose and praying to avoid any sensors. She was taller than she wanted to be, and in lesser shape than she liked these days. She'd quit soccer when she came out because her school wouldn't let her play on the girl's team. She did not miss the men's locker room, but she missed playing center-forward.

None of the bots paused. A mostly-healed burn on her left shoulder reminded her not to let them detect her this time. Every last one came equipped with weaponry beyond reason.

Up close, the DragonCycle™ logo's pale yellow lettering and black outline was more visible on the sides of the boxes, and emblazoned on every bot. Candace winced at the sight. They were the latest online service by Dragon.river, Inc.. Online customers designed their bikes with the help of a seamless design program, and Dragon shipped the parts to their door with a one-use ConBot to put it all together. For every unit purchased, a bike was donated to a nonspecific "third world country."

Candace took careful steps towards the door on the wall she was up against. Without pushing, she turned the knob slowly, and when she was sure the latch bolt was out of the way, she moved the door and entered the storage room.

This room was even bigger and darker than the loading room. The aisles of boxes faded quickly in the shadows, giving them the impression of being endless. Bots flew through the aisles, placing boxes into a larger box to be loaded onto the conveyor belt.

Slipping into the closest aisle, Candace peered at the boxes, arranged in a seemingly random order. Pedal, handlebars, forks, stem, shifter, etc. Boxes of each kind were uniform, so she would have to do some reading to find a rear derailleur.

It was the last part she needed for her bootleg bike.

She spotted a box—a row higher than she could reach—that she thought might be the derailleur. With her right hand, she pulled herself up just enough to snag it from the shelf, careful to grab it with only her fingers to avoid setting off the PushPalm.

Most of her bike was not stolen. She'd found the frame with most of the necessary parts in a junkyard, but it had taken work and a little bit of petty theft to replace a few of the damaged or missing parts. Maia had helped with a few of the cons. DragonCycles™ had particular, trademarked parts, so they had to go into the more affluent suburbs nearby and lift a tire and a seat, among other things. The rear derailleur on her junkyard bike was rusted and busted pretty bad, and removing it from a stranger's bike would not be as quick as the other parts had been. Not to mention, those affluent suburbanites had bolstered their WatchBots since noticing the string of missing bike parts. Candace insisted they take only one part per bike. It would be easier for their targets to replace.

"Their parents will buy them replacements before the end of the day," Maia had assured.

Usually, she took the distraction/lookout position, while Candace fiddled with the bikes to remove the desired parts. Then Maia's bike, saved from her parent's closing shop, served as the getaway, with Candace standing on the pegs, holding Maia's shoulders. But the area was littered with hills, and Maia flat out refused to bike up any of those with a whole extra person on the bike.

"We're like Bonnie and Clyde," Maia had said as they sat behind an ice cream shop, waiting for a mark to roll by.

"I don't know if that fits," Candace had said, turning a wrench over in her hand. "Didn't they kill people?"

"Ok. We're like if Bonnie and Clyde didn't kill people." Maia turned to kiss Candace's forehead.

"And we're queer as hell."

"That, too."

The box was light, no more than a pound. She flipped it over to read it. Rear Derailleur. She had her boon, and she broke into a cautious stride toward the door she'd come in through.

Back in the loading area, Candace tossed the box from hand to hand, approaching the spot she'd initially landed in. She thought about how she would have to position herself to fire a pulse from the PushPalm to propel her out the window without misjudging the shot. As she thought, the package landed on the switch beside her index knuckle. A wave of force propelled it across the room.

Every single bot froze in place, most of them hanging on the electric charges projected through the air, so they seemed to be suspended underwater. Candace tried to freeze, too, but her heart was punching her ribs, her lungs burning. The derailleur was sitting on the floor in the middle of the room. If she abandoned it, she couldn't finish her bike, and she certainly couldn't give this a second shot. Security would be heightened for a year. Every bot turned to face her. Before any of them moved, she leapt over the halted conveyor belt and sprinted toward the box.

Bots fired yellow-hot lasers in every direction, but Candace was quick to leap and roll out of the way. She restructured her trajectory so she would curve toward the box and continue her route to turn back toward the window.

She swiped the box and made for her escape. A line of bots floated in front of the window, but this was actually beneficial. Candace leaped up and used each bot as a step to the window. She barrelled through it, pointing her PushPalm back and firing to propel herself further and faster. She landed with a skid that broke skin on her knees and elbows, but she jumped up and ran, box in hand. On the street, Maia was waiting, poised to pedal. Candace hopped on the pegs without a thought, and they took off.

At home, Candace led Maia into the garage. Candace's right knee was bleeding, but no more than a bad shaving cut. She plopped on the ground beside her bike, and picked up her ratty copy of *Plume and Granby's Encyclopedia of Bicycle Anatomy*. The book weighed as much as her bike, and had information on every model and part imaginable. She turned to the page about rear derailleurs and got to work. Maia dabbed Candace's wounds with a towel, then got out some old cans of blue and yellow spray paint. By the next morning, the bike was finished, the frame's yellow

DragonCycle™ logo and design gone. Flecks of paint speckled the bike's tires, chain, and grip. The frame was black with messy stripes of pink and purple, and "BONNIE" written in red.

THE DRAGON'S LAKE

Sarena Ulibarri

L ita crawled out of the cave mouth and rolled onto her back on the soft ground. So much for the quest to find the missing princess. So much for the gold and glory and whatever else she'd been promised. When the sinkhole had opened up, her fingers had slipped right out of Coran's. Or had Coran let her go? She supposed it didn't matter now. Coran and the others were long gone, and Lita was still alive. If she could stay alive, she could crawl home—to what was left of home, anyway.

Her eyes adjusted to the light after days—weeks?—in the dark cave. The sky was the purple of sunset. *More darkness*, Lita thought with despair. At least the two moons would give off more light than the phosphorescent rocks and glow of amphibious eyes that had been her only company in the cave. She rolled to her side, pine needles stabbing her arms, and pushed herself up. If she could get oriented, she could head toward home. But a smell permeated the air . . . *food*. And sounds . . . *laughter, conversation*.

Lita stumbled between the trees, her mouth watering from the scent of roasted peppers and lamb's meat. Maybe she was closer to home than she realized, if that's what was being cooked. Candlelight flickered in the darkness, illuminating a long table. People dressed in fine long robes and glittering jewelry were seated before rows of elaborate dishes. Lita balked—she was a mess from being trapped in the cave without her pack, and if she went wandering in there like a beggar they might send her away or even kill her. Surely a soirée in the woods like this had armed guards to keep these beautiful people safe.

But then one of them spotted her, a woman with golden brown skin and sleek dark hair. She smiled radiantly and beckoned Lita forward, each gesture exaggerated by the trail of her white flowing sleeve. That wasn't . . . it couldn't be.

No, but she *looked* like Devony. Her lovely Devony, who had left Lita after the Wingstead fire just months before. The others turned toward her too, raised their glasses, and smiled.

Just before she should have reached the clearing, the whole scene disappeared. The tantalizing scents were gone, replaced by a musty, fishy smell. Where the table had been there was now a small lake, dotted with islands. A short-haired woman in plain gray clothes looked up from a fish basket.

"Oh no," she said when she saw Lita.

Lita stumbled back the way she'd come, but though she could see the forest beyond, it was as though looking at it through a glass wall. A discordant whistle ripped through the air, and then something sticky and flexible seized her arm. She turned back just long enough to see the eyestalks of a giant snail, and then something pinched her arm—a bite? a needle?—and everything went dark.

· · ·

No more purple sky. Lita awoke to the glow of fire and lurched urgently to her feet. The room swam around her, slowly coming into focus. No, this was not the fire that had ripped through her laboratory and consumed half of Wingstead. This fire blazed controlled in two torches on either side of a . . . She bolted backward.

A dragon grinned at her, reptilian lips pulled up over daggers of teeth. The creature's body coiled snake-like on the stone floor.

"Welcome home," the dragon said.

Lita looked for an exit but the room seemed made of shadows.

"This is not my home."

"It is now. Don't worry. Your every need will be met, so long as mine are."

He lifted his tail, thick at the base and split into two sharpened tips, and flicked it toward a table. Not quite as elaborate as the one in the forest, but well-stocked with grilled fish and fruits. Lita rushed to the table, her stomach rumbling. Her hand halfway toward the first bite, she paused. The food could be poisoned. Or accepting it could be some sort of contract.

As though sensing the reasons for her hesitation, the dragon's tail reached all the way to the table and speared a fish. He tossed it through the air and caught it in snapping jaws.

"You are trapped here, I think you already know that. But don't worry, you'll grow comfortable."

Lita hesitated a moment longer, then ate a few handfuls. The knot of hunger loosened and the world became clearer. She wiped her mouth with the back of her hand.

"I will not serve you," she said. "Let me go."

The dragon uncoiled and slithered across the floor until his face loomed above her. He sniffed exaggeratedly, huge nostrils widening and then contracting.

"I like you, but I could kill you just as easily. I do grow tired of fish and fowl. We shall see if you end up serving dinner, or being it. Tok!"

Lita flinched at this last exclamation. A large snail glided out of the shadows, moving toward her on one rippling muscular foot. Its spiral shell rose to the height of her chest, and its eyestalks towered a few hand-spans above her head.

"Yes, exalted one." The snail spoke in a double voice, an uncomfortable mix of high and low pitches, as though it were working with two separate vocal organs to approximate speech.

"Time to show our newest resident to her quarters."

A sticky appendage wrapped around Lita's arm again and she braced for the sharp bite, but this time it did not come. A door appeared out of nowhere, and the snail dragged her out of the shadowy room.

Outside, the air sang with insects and night birds. Floral scents mingled with the musty fish smell she'd first noticed. The snail guided her away from the tower on the lake's shore, crossing a bridge to a small island, then over two more until they reached an island that held only a circular wooden hut with a rag-covered doorway. Inside, the snail made an inexplicable sound, which activated an orb glowing in the center of the ceiling. People stirred from bunks along the wall—all women, Lita noted with some relief. They started to get up, but when the snail said, "Newbie," they crawled back into their bunks.

"There's a free bed over here," said the short-haired woman Lita had first seen at the lake's edge. The woman smiled sadly at Lita and pointed to the bunk above hers. The snail pushed Lita toward it. She climbed the ladder into the bunk and then lay staring at the ceiling, wondering just what she'd stumbled into.

·　　　·　　　·

The work was hot, but not especially hard. There were around thirty other humans, more women than men. The men repaired the bridges that connected the dozen or so small islands in the dragon's lake, or else swam with large buckets of soil to a mound that was apparently a new island under construction. The women cleared weeds from the island shores, which teemed with vines and bright pink and orange flowers, scrubbed algae from the outer stones of the dragon's tower, and cooked meals to serve to the dragon and snails, keeping whatever was left for the humans. Everyone fished. The snails ordered them around from shady alcoves where a few favored humans fanned them with palm fronds and periodically doused their skin with fresh lake water.

Lita wandered to the shore of the lake several times, and no one bothered to stop her. She could get to the trees and brambles that surrounded the lake, but always ran into that invisible wall. If Coran had been here, she would have known what sort of an enchantment it was, maybe even how to defeat it. But Coran and the rest of the group she'd ventured out with were far away, had probably already found the missing princess and moved on to the next adventure. Lita was an alchemist, and without at least the tool kit that had been lost in the sinkhole, her skills were useless. She constantly picked up rocks, searching for some recognizable mineral that she could use, picked at berries and flowers, but so far everything in the dragon's lake was innocuous.

On her third night in this strange prison, Lita heard a tap on the bunk bed and saw the corner of a tablet sticking up along the wall. The other humans had generally ignored her. She had begun to wonder if they were drugged or hypnotized. She pulled the tablet up, angling it to catch a stream of moonlight in order to read.

What's your name?

Lita took the small nub of chalk strapped to the board. She wrote *Lita*, then paused, and added, *2nd-born of the Phantom House, in Wingstead*. The city of Wingstead was nearly gone now, burned by the fire that had begun next door and grew to uncontrollable proportions when it hit the explosive chemicals in her laboratory. But Phantom House still meant something to those who knew the ranks of nobility in lands beyond this one. Wherever *this one* was.

She tapped the bunk and passed the tablet back down. It came back a moment later with the message, *I'm Kass.*

Just "Kass." No indications of homeland or birth order to help Lita understand how she fit into the world. Her handwriting indicated a classical training, but that didn't really reveal much.

It means "blackbird" where I'm from, Lita wrote back.

Yes, where I'm from too, the return message said, which narrowed things down only a little.

Lita started to scratch another message, but the ceiling orb lit up, and the snail's weird polyphonic voice said, "Get up, get up, time to choose." Lita shoved the tablet under the blanket.

"Up, up, everyone pretty."

Lita tentatively crawled down the ladder and stood next to Kass, who didn't lift her eyes, even when Lita whispered, "What's going on?"

Two snails flanked a man, who stood in the doorway, glancing around nervously. "Choose," one snail commanded. He glanced at the half-circle of women, and Lita's mouth went dry as she realized what was going on. She stepped backward, bumping into the ladder. He lifted a hand to point toward a red-headed woman near the doorway.

"Please," she said softly, "I'm with the greater moon."

"I'll take a go at him," said an older woman with stringy, waist-length hair, making a lewd gesture. A few of them laughed. The others bowed their heads even lower, seeming to sink into themselves. The man looked over Kass, then Lita, who narrowed her eyes at him. She didn't sleep with men, and no cultish sex-show was going to change that. His gaze finally landed on someone else, who stepped forward and went with him. The snails barked orders to return to bed.

Shaken, Lita crawled back into the bunk, and flinched at the hard edge of the tablet she'd forgotten was there. With trembling fingers, she wrote, *Has anyone ever gotten out of here?* She passed it down to Kass, but didn't get a response.

·   ·   ·

Lita lowered a basket of fish and wiped the sweat from her forehead. She was on the outer shore of the lake, near the invisible shield that threatened to make this her permanent life. One of the snails glided past her, toward the barrier.

And went straight through it.

Lita stood sharply. Over the last several days, she'd traced the perimeter, memorized exactly which trees or shrubs were beyond the barrier, and this snail had gone straight past it, she was sure. She charged toward the same spot. Her hand hit first, and then her nose, and she stumbled backward with an electric shock. The snail looked back over its shell at her and gave a nightmarish double-voiced cackle.

Lita sat staring at the barrier for the next hour. Once, a snail yelled at her to get to work, but did nothing to enforce it. She watched as a couple of blackbirds darted in and out of the barrier, catching flying insects. A salamander bumped up against the barrier and skirted along its perimeter before giving up and sliding back into the water. Was it an issue of height? That didn't explain the snail, but she climbed a tree anyway, pounding against the enchantment until the shocks nearly numbed her arm.

The thin branches snapped beneath her weight and she tumbled to the ground. She lay there, trying to ignore the pain radiating from her bruised hip, watching the birds pass through the enchantment as though it weren't even there.

Kass appeared above her and Lita sat up, pulling grass out of her hair. She'd landed in mud, apparently, and it painted her whole left sleeve red.

"If you don't work, they won't let you eat," Kass said.

"I don't want to eat. I want to leave."

"I want to go home too. But only the snails can leave."

Lita gave up on brushing the mud off. It was already starting to dry in the warm air, so she tried to peel it from her hands instead.

"Yes, but *why* can the snails leave?"

Kass shrugged. "They serve the dragon. He's convinced them that if they work for him, they will eventually be allowed to transform into dragons themselves, complete with all his magic."

"Is it true?"

"I have no idea. I suspect not. They're probably just as much slaves as we are."

Lita shook her head. It didn't matter, and she wasn't about to start feeling sympathy for her captors.

"But the snails *aren't* the only ones who can pass through. Look."

Lita pointed to the birds. Then, in a low voice, she said, "I think maybe the enchantment is limited by mode of locomotion." She'd remembered Coran talking about something like this near the beginning of their quest. "Anything that walks or crawls on legs can't pass through, but if you could fly, or glide—"

"Or roll?" Kass asked suddenly.

"Uh, maybe, yeah. Then the barrier lets you through." Lita had seen the flying machines people used to soar off the Great Cliffs outside of Wingstead, but she didn't know the mechanics behind them. And there was a potion she'd studied that could make one float, though the ingredients were unlikely to be found in the lake. Still, it was possible.

"Come here, I want to show you something." Kass offered her hand. Lita brushed away the last bits of mud she could manage and took her hand, hefting herself up.

Kass led her in silence around the edge of the lake. When she saw the tower where the dragon lived, she balked, wondering if this was a trick. Would Kass turn her in for searching for an escape route, gain some kind of favor from the dragon that way? But Kass beckoned toward a stand of trees near the perimeter, and lifted a fallen branch to reveal something Lita had certainly not expected to see: a wheel. Kass checked for onlookers, then pulled the branches back a little more. The contraption resembled half a horse-drawn wagon, but had handlebars and a seat more like the flying machines. Yet it had no wings.

"What is it?" Lita asked.

"You've never seen a bicycle before?"

Lita shook her head.

"You pedal to make the wheels roll." Kass kicked a pedal in demonstration, and the back wheel turned, catching in the branches that had lodged between the spokes.

Lita's eyes widened. "We should try it."

Kass lowered the branches back over the machine and pulled Lita's arm to lead her away. "It's broken. The fork that holds the front wheel in place is snapped in half, and the rim is badly bent."

"But we could fix it."

"Maybe we could fix it," Kass agreed.

·   ·   ·

Over the next week, Lita and Kass discussed possible ways to mend or replace the fork. Lita found a sturdy branch that was the right shape, and

Kass gathered scraps that might be useful for attaching it. A couple of screws stolen from the legs of a table, some bits of rope from a broken basket, a step pulled from the ladder of their bunk. They passed designs back and forth on Kass's tablet until they'd worn the bit of chalk to a sliver.

Once more, the snails arrived with a man in the middle of the night, this one less timid and more boastful, dragging an unwilling woman away. Some kind of breeding program, Kass finally explained. Lita had seen no babies or pregnant bellies since she'd been here, but perhaps it was only a matter of time.

The first time they went out to the hiding place to work on the bicycle, Lita managed to straighten the rim by stomping on it and bending it over a rock, but the branch Kass tried to attach as a makeshift fork broke. They found a stronger one and returned the next night to try again. It held, but then they had to figure out how to address the flattened tires. Using a mash of mud and reeds to stuff the tires seemed to do the trick. Finally, Kass balanced the bicycle and rode a loop around the stand of trees. Lita raised her fists in victory, then frowned as Kass brought the bicycle to a stop in front of her.

"It's only designed to hold one person, isn't it?"

"It might work with two," Kass said, and described how Lita could balance on the handlebars.

They tried, but Lita was both taller and heavier than Kass, and kept knocking the balance off to the side. Eventually she knocked them over so badly they collapsed into a giggling pile, and Kass lay with her arm across Lita's waist. It felt nice, the soft warmth of her, the pleasant tickle of her hair, but lying there like that with Kass only made Lita miss Devony even more. She rolled away and sat up.

A light came on in the dragon's tower and the two clambered up and hid the bicycle, then ducked behind the trees. A snail crossed the bridge to the dragon's tower, a body draped across its shell, this one a boy of twelve or so, still dressed in his own clothing.

"Another new one," Kass whispered once the snail was inside. "Come on, we have to get back to the bunks."

They crept quietly through the flowers and across the bridges until they reached the women's hut. Once there, Kass passed the tablet up with the message, *You will have to ride.* There was no more chalk left to write a response.

· · ·

It took three more nights of practice for Lita to achieve a confident balance on the bicycle, under Kass's patient, sometimes not-so-patient, tutelage. They only had one chance to get this right, if it was even going to work at all. If she crashed or stepped a foot down at just the wrong moment, the barrier would block them.

"I don't know if I can do this," Lita said after she'd toppled Kass from the handlebars for the fourth time that night.

"These rubbish tires and bent rim aren't doing you any favors," Kass said, "but you're learning faster than I did, and I first rode on smooth marble floors, with a technician nearby to fix any little flaw. A few more tries will do it, I'm sure."

Smooth marble floors? Even Phantom House, where she'd grown up, had rough-shod cobblestone, not smooth marble floors. That must mean that Kass—

A polyphonic shriek interrupted her revelation.

"Out of bed, out of bed, two missing," a snail's cry carried across the lake, picked up and repeated by several others.

"Oh no," Kass groaned.

They must have stopped by the women's hut for another "choosing" and found two of their potential stock missing. Snails and humans emerged, the islands lighting up with orbs. A torch flared to life inside the dragon's tower.

"Lita," Kass said, looking fervently into her eyes. "It's now or never."

Lita nodded, and climbed on the bicycle. Kass balanced in front of her. With a deep breath, she pushed off, pedaling them toward the barrier.

Lita wobbled, but kept pedaling. They passed through. The discordant shrieks of the snails grew louder behind them.

"That way, that way, there's a trail," Kass shouted.

She could barely see enough to avoid smashing into the trees, but Lita turned the way Kass pointed, nearly tumbled again, and found a rocky trough that must be the trail.

"No, up, not down," Kass yelled again. Lita did knock her off this time, barely catching herself as she turned the bicycle around. While Kass resettled herself, Lita glanced back. Silhouettes of three snails charged toward them.

"I thought snails were supposed to be slow!" Lita wheezed. These seemed to practically float, each slimy foot rippling to propel them across the forest floor. Lita pushed, standing on the pedals to get more power up the hill. Her heart pounded, and her lungs burned. The wheel hit a rock and the bicycle toppled, spilling both of them.

"Take it," Lita said, and shoved the handlebars toward Kass. "You know how to ride, you can go faster on your own."

"I'm not leaving you."

"Go. I'll run behind."

Kass hesitated, then righted the bicycle and climbed on. Lita pushed herself to her feet and ran. Kass disappeared into the forest ahead of her. The snails grew closer behind her. Lita followed the trail. One more step, one more step: that's all she could focus on. One more, and one more after that.

Firelight blazed through the trees ahead of her, and Lita balked, remembering the illusion that had drawn her into the dragon's lake in the first place. But she'd managed to leave the snails behind, or they'd given up on her, so she pressed forward, bursting out of the trees.

Right into a squadron of bayonets, pointed at her face. Lita skidded to a stop, hands raised.

"No, wait." It was Kass's voice. "That's my rescuer."

Breathless, confused, half-terrified, Lita still managed to breathe out, "Ha! Hardly."

The guards lowered their weapons and Lita saw Kass standing in the doorway of the guard turret, her bicycle against the wall. One of the guards had given her his coat, and she looked even smaller with it on.

Smaller, yes, but certainly not frail or weak.

Behind Kass, against the lightening sky, loomed the outline of Blackbird Castle.

· · ·

Princess Melikasha was welcomed home with tears and trumpets. Lita was offered a chest of gold and jewels for her safe return—the same prize she and Coran and the others had gone out for in the first place. The queen sent a messenger to track down Lita's former party, who had clearly gone searching in the wrong direction.

The princess hadn't been kidnapped by trolls or run off with the Duke of a different castle after all. She'd gone riding her bicycle into the nearby woods and been snared by a selfish dragon.

Once the fanfare wore down, Lita approached Melikasha. Her hair was clean and slicked back now, curling slightly at the nape of her neck, and she was dressed more like a warrior than like royalty. The contour-fitting leather pants and bodice suited her much better than the flowing robes and gowns would have. Lita had been offered similar garb, in the lighter grays and browns more appropriate for someone of Phantom House than the striking blacks and purples of Blackbird Castle.

"My lady," Lita said, kneeling before her.

"Ha," Kass said. "Don't you dare 'my lady' me. Get up. We're equals."

Though she appreciated the sentiment, Lita knew it was not true. Still, she rose and looked her friend in the eye.

"There's a place for you here," Kass said. "If you would like to stay at Blackbird Castle."

The offer was tempting, but Lita couldn't say yes or no right now. The quest she'd set off on was technically complete, but the one she'd found herself in wasn't quite resolved.

"The others out there in the dragon's lake . . . we can't just leave them out there."

"I agree," Kass said, and beckoned her toward the window. They looked out on a courtyard where a dozen artisans constructed bicycles.

Lita frowned. "But the enchantment may have been modified after we escaped."

"Sounds like you need someone who knows about enchantments, then." They both whirled at the sound of the new voice.

Coran leaned against the doorway, picking at her nails. And Stararm and Howler too, lurking just outside.

"We heard about your little detour," Coran said.

Relief warred with resentment.

"You let go of me in the sinkhole," Lita said, her hands balling into fists.

"No she didn't," Howler said. "She cried for three days when we thought you were dead."

Coran punched him in the shoulder so hard he stumbled backward.

"Ow!" he complained.

"You really thought I let you go on purpose?"

"Figured you couldn't wait to be rid of me."

Coran looked sheepish for a moment, and Lita released her fists. Kass leaned against the window, a slight smile playing at her lips. Lita wished she and Coran could have this conversation in private, but of course Coran had to have an audience for everything.

"I know I always gave you a hard time, but I didn't let go. I wouldn't do that. You're part of our team."

"Aww!" Stararm crooned, and then gave an exaggerated flinch as Coran shot him a look. "It's true, though," he said to Lita with a wink.

Lita wanted to believe it. Coran had always come across as an arrogant hardass, but maybe there was more to the woman than she'd known.

"I'm glad you're not dead," Coran said after an awkward silence.

"Yeah, well, me too," Lita said.

Coran put her bravado back on like slipping on a mask. "But, you haven't *really* saved the princess until you've defeated the dragon, have you?"

·　　　·　　　·

Lita rode a bicycle towing a wagon of other bicycles into the forest. Kass rode another one. At first, the queen had forbidden her to go with them, but Kass had fought back, and there she was. Coran, Howler, Stararm, and two of the castle guards were with them. Using the alchemist's laboratory at Blackbird Castle, Lita had finally been able to put her skills to use, mixing the wall-smashing powders that filled the grenades she carried in a bag at her side.

When they reached the barrier, rather than the inviting dinner scene that had lured Lita in, two dozen fierce warriors wearing skull helmets and wielding sparking spears blocked their path. The others raised their weapons, but Coran lifted a hand to signal them to wait. She stepped forward.

"Amateurs," she muttered as she painted a sigil in the air. Then, "Hmm, okay," when one of the illusive warriors struck it away. She tried a different one and the warriors all froze, spears held in mid-strike, faces immobile. Coran walked right through one of the warriors like it was a translucent ghost. The others followed, passing through the veil of the illusion. The dragon's lake appeared before them.

"Huh, it's pretty!" Coran said. "Doesn't seem like the worst place to be trapped by an evil dragon."

Lita and Kass glared at her.

Gray-robed people looked up from their work, confused at the sudden arrival of the entourage. Snails charged forward, and were met with salt guns that left them shriveled, shrieking messes. Some of the people fought back too, because they didn't understand. Kass caught one of the women, who Lita recognized from a bunk near theirs, and showed her the bicycles, explaining how they could get through the barrier. Lita ran across the network of bridges to catch up with the rest of her party at the dragon's tower on the other side of the lake.

From the bridge, she hurled a grenade toward the tiny window in the closest turret. The wall of the tower exploded, raining stone and debris down on them. Through the dust, the dragon curled up, whipping his head side to side. Howler and Stararm readied their spears, Coran prepared a spell, and Lita gripped another grenade. The dragon roared at them, but rather than charge, it dove back down into the tower and disappeared.

The party waited a moment, glancing awkwardly at each other. Finally, Lita crossed the bridge, grenade still in hand, and climbed over the crumbling wall.

The dragon was gone. Lita peered down into a gaping hole in the tower's floor, one that hadn't been formed by the grenade. Coran shined a light down into it, illuminating the curve of stalactites and the glitter of gypsum. It was the same uncharted cave system where Lita had been lost before finding her way to the lake in the first place.

"He'll find new victims," Lita said.

"Surely," Coran agreed. "But these ones will be able to move on."

They stepped out of the crumbling tower. Along the perimeter of the lake, people were tottering on the bicycles and rolling out into the forest.

"You know," Coran said. "If you wanted to come with us on the next quest, I guess it would be okay."

Lita put the un-thrown grenade back in the pouch. She'd left Wingstead because each charred building, each half-burnt field reminded her of what she'd lost. Although the fire had not really been her fault, Devony had blamed her and so had many of the villagers, needing somewhere to anchor their grief. But in leaving with Coran, trying to live this wayfaring life she really wasn't suited to, had she really been moving on, or had she just been running away?

Kass waved, shouting something that was just out of earshot and pointing toward the barrier, which appeared to be losing strength the farther away the dragon got. Eventually it would fail and everyone would be able to walk out. Lita glanced at Coran, and shrugged, trying to mimic her nonchalance.

"I guess I could," she said. "But . . ." Lita looked back towards Kass. "I think you helped me get right to where I need to be."

Coran patted her on the back and they crossed the bridge to help the remaining captives of dragon's lake find their freedom.

STORING TREASURES

Paul Abbamondi

THE
END

'TIL WE MEET AGAIN

Joyce Chng

The road to Cage City is fraught with danger. Stim-crazy nuts wait to ambush the racers with their dragon bikes so that they can sell the bikes to feed their habit. Rogue trainers wait to befriend young wannabes, fresh on the scene and too innocent to know the difference between caring and creepy. All these Meiki avoids, taking a different route with her dragon bike, coursing through the coarse canyon ravines and plains instead, reveling in the freedom and the sheer sense of adventure of traveling.

Her dragon bike loves the open spaces too, its throaty growls coming forth from its engine. Meiki's gloved hands grip the handlebars tightly, a little possessively. Curved like horns, with gleaming chrome coating, the dragon-head front of the bike cuts through the air, the fierce eyes daring anyone to cross its path. Meiki laughs with the wind as it roars in her and through her.

"Does it have a name?" her grandmother asked before she set off on the journey to Cage City. They had dotted the lamp-eyes with blessed black ink. The dragon bike stood right in the middle of the workshop, glowing under the cone of the flashlight. It looked wicked, all sleek curves and polished flanks. The wheels were microfiber wheels, designed to withstand all sorts of stress. As per the tradition of her dragon clan, it had the hint of green, like the faintest peridot merged within the silver chrome. "It needs to have a name in order to be alive."

"It has a name, ah-ma," Meiki said, staring indulgently at her dragon bike.

Racing is the purview of all dragon clans. In the past, they rode real dragons, but Federation policy had made dragons a protected species. All the rookies shut down. The clan matriarchs found bike-racing a viable alternative to flying and soon, workshops opened everywhere in the Federation. They came up with their own traditions and rules when it came to making the dragon bikes, right down to the dotting of the dragon eyes.

The naming of the dragon bike has roots in the naming of the dragon, when the rider is paired with a suitable dragon. The real dragons, rainbow-feathered and sleek, spoke in color tones. Their names were also color-related. Dragon bikes also have names that draw inspiration from their immediate surroundings. So, her dragon bike is Sun Silver, because the golden sun lanced through the cracks in the workshop that fateful day.

Her ah-ma is one of the last dragon racers. She still has vid pics plastered all over the workshop. A young, dark-haired woman smiling victoriously, her dragon rearing beside her, in an obviously posed publicity vidshot. Another pic of the same young woman, holding up the winning garland. Her grandmother had short hair and a cocky grin. Her dragon had bright eyes and large sail-like wings.

Sun Silver leaps across the small ravines and creeks lacing across the canyon floor. Meiki holds onto the handlebars. The air tastes of rosemary and sharper-tasting desert plants. Cage City is in sight. The towers and the roof of the Arena are seen, stabbing up into the sky. She can now compete in the Grand Prix and win honor for her dragon clan.

· · ·

Cage City is a riot of colors and sounds. It is half-clan and half-City folk. The division can be seen in how they designed the City. The gigantic Arena, shaped like a cage, is in the center of the City. Colorful banners fly in the strong wind, the colors of all the competing clans and even some of the City families. She sees the green of her clan and feels the immense pride rise in her chest. The sense of pride dissipates a little as Sun Silver enters the gate and Meiki feels eyes and all optics focus on her. Cage City loves gossip and betting. Eager punters want to know who to bet their money on. She presses the throttle, feeling Sun Silver respond to the cue. She later finds the rest stop for the night, right next to the Racing Arena. The expenses have already been keyed into the system. She only has to park Sun Silver in the designated berth.

The rest stop has delicious handmade noodles. Meiki slurps the entire bowl and goes to bed, content.

She wakes up at dawn to train. Already she hears the deep throbbing roars and growls of other dragon bikes. She has a quick breakfast of hot rice and sour pickles before running to Sun Silver's berth. After fuelling Sun Silver, she heads to the Arena.

Racers from all the clans are there. Here a racer from the Fire Drake clan, looking as if she is only ten, whizzing down the lane with a practiced ease. There a girl from the Wolf Dragon clan, with a beautifully crafted jet-colored dragon bike, going through her paces. All the competitors look extremely good.

Meiki can see the ten race banners in vivid yellow and gold arranged around the circuit. "In the past," her grandmother said when they rested between tinkering with Sun Silver's engines and valves, "we had to capture all the banners in order to win. It wasn't just finishing the circuit, but collecting the banners. Miss one and you are immediately disqualified. I believe they changed the rules now."

She rides around the circuit, feeling her way around the unfamiliar terrain. The floor isn't even. Cage City has constructed the Arena quickly, in the hopes of cashing in on the dragon bikes. Sun Silver doesn't seem to mind, its growls deep and filled with a primal gusto. She sometimes wonders if the dragon bikes have been infused with the spirits of real dragons.

Someone screams, followed by a lot of shouting and swearing. She smells the burnt odor of burning synthetics and brakes hard. A few lengths before her, a dragon bike has caught fire. The racer has fortunately leapt out and is currently crying on the grass verge. The girl looks about her age and has the bearing of a Major Clan scion. The race marshals and medics rush over, extinguishing the fire and checking the girl all over for injuries. Now she looks more angry than upset. All the racers have paused in their training. A dragon bike gone. An entire year's worth of training and investment gone.

Meiki catches the girl's eyes. They are furious. It must be humiliating too. Meiki feels helpless. The race marshals tow the dragon bike away, the girl following them with a numb expression, her arms wrapped around her body as if she is cold.

Troubled, Meiki finishes her training and retires back to the rest stop for the night's Grand Prix. Already, punters are streaming into the arena, grabbing the best seats before the entire place fills up later.

·　　　·　　　·

"It's sabotage," a familiar voice greets Meiki when she walks into the dining space of the rest stop. She has heard the voice before, at the Arena. "It's sabotage and you know it, Aunt!"

The girl she saw back at the Arena is gesticulating angrily at an older woman. They are wearing the crimson red of a Major Clan. Radiant Claws? Meiki glances quickly at the badges on their chests: a white claw.

"Calm down, Leizhu." The older woman has the same placating voice as Meiki's own aunts when they try to smooth things over in the clan. "Don't jump to conclusions just yet."

"I heard another girl had the exact same problem," Leizhu isn't placated. "Broke down in the middle of the race track. Mechanic couldn't find anything."

Meiki grabs her lunch and settles down to eat. She is surprised when Leizhu sits down beside her.

"Saw you at the track," is all Leizhu says as a greeting. "You look like a friendly face I can talk to."

"I am sorry it happened," Meiki says. The mixed rice is so delicious. It reminds her of home.

Leizhu stabs her bowl of rice with her chopsticks. "I still think it's sabotage. The circuit has grown dishonest, many clans greedy for prestige. I am Leizhu, by the way."

"I am Meiki."

"You have a beautiful dragon bike," Leizhu says, smiling. All anger seems gone from her.

Meiki feels a rush of pride. "Thank you." *And yours too, before it caught fire*, she adds silently in her head.

"I am not sure I will race tonight," Leizhu shakes her head. She has a quiet sense of beauty about her. "My aunt promises we have a spare bike in our carrier . . . But it's nothing without Gold Star."

They eat quietly, enjoying their newfound companionship. Then, Leizhu's aunt appears again, her face suddenly stern. Leizhu rolls her eyes, puts away her bowl and utensil at the counter, and lingers a little longer at the table before she follows her aunt out.

"See you soon, I hope," Leizhu says with a wink before walking out of the dining hall.

Meiki shivers. The talk about sabotage frightens her. She has heard rumors about such things back home. Intuition pricks at her and she finds herself at Sun Silver's berth. Her heart plunges when she sees a pool of dark oil forming beneath Sun Silver's engines. Someone has opened the valve-cap, allowing the fuel to leak out. Fuelling the dragon bike will take one hour. Not enough time before the Grand Prix starts.

A noise startles her and Meiki jumps, almost dropping the nozzle. The Wolf Dragon racer she saw at the training ground, the one with the beautifully crafted dragon bike, is standing there. Her expression reminds Meiki of a rat caught eating rice in her clan's kitchen.

"YOU!" Meiki yells. "You are the one sabotaging all the bikes!"

Frightened, the girl turns around and runs. Meiki dashes after her, yelling "Saboteur! Saboteur!" Fortunately, when she reaches the end of the corridor, a burly Security woman has grabbed hold of the struggling girl. "She's the one sabotaging the bikes," Meiki snarls.

"You are going to the cages, girl!" The Security woman snaps and ties the girl's hands with wire. "A complaint will be filed to your Clan and a Black Mark will be given. Silence!" The girl gives up struggling, staring into thin air glumly.

As the woman leads the criminal away, Meiki races back to Sun Silver. She has some time left. She tries to fix the valve with epoxy. The leak stops. She isn't sure how long it can last.

She is going to race without a full tank. Meiki tries to dispel the fear inside her. She feels cold. She is frightened that she is going to fail her grandmother and her clan. She sticks the refuel nozzle into the dragon bike, her heart pumping hard.

Meiki manages to get the tank to almost full before the bell rings for all the bikers to assemble at the arena. She bites her lower lip.

Hope the epoxy holds, she prays fervently.

·　　·　　·

Meiki sends a message off to her clan via the vid-system before donning her racing leathers. She wears the green of her clan with pride and dons her badge solemnly. She will deal with grandmother's reply later.

The crowd roars like a flight of dragons when she emerges out into the open with Sun Silver. The sound is at once deafening and exhilarating. Her blood begins to pump. Her heart beats like a drum. Overnight, the adverts flash and shimmer. Around her, the spectators merge into one sea of waving flags.

"I heard you caught the saboteur!" Leizhu's voice is almost drowned with another burst of cheering. She stands beside Meiki, waving to the crowd. She's obviously one of the crowd favorites. Radiant Claws is a popular Clan.

"You are riding Gold Star?" Meiki waves to the crowd, heading towards the starting line. She is still worried about Sun Silver. Can the dragon bike last through the entire race? She is envious of Leizhu, so composed and calm. Meiki also can't explain the surge of happiness when she sees the girl. *She's my competitor*, Meiki feels her cheeks flushing with heat. *My competitor!*

"Fixed," Leizhu grins. "I insisted. The damage wasn't that bad. I couldn't bear sitting on a dragon bike not attuned to me."

"When we rode dragons," grandmother told Meiki on the day of Mid-Autumn Moon, when they hung lanterns across the courtyard and ate sweet baked pastry filled with lotus seed paste. "We understood them, because we had a special bond. One rider was attuned to her dragon and vice versa. I can't explain the bond, child. Friendship? Kinship? All apply and are the same."

Other riders appear with their dragon bikes. The Wolf Dragon racer wasn't amongst them. The crowd booed at the remaining Wolf Dragon representatives watching in the galley. News had gotten out fast.

"May the best racer win!" Leizhu salutes jauntily, exchanging a fist bump with Meiki. Meiki beams. Her heart swells. Perhaps the feeling *is* mutual. Meiki settles comfortably on Sun Silver's seat, feeling the throaty growl of the dragon bike. She remembers that she's racing without a full tank and determination grows inside her.

"Perhaps, when the Grand Prix is over, we can meet up for some tea and sweet dim sum," the Radiant Claws girl whispers before she pulls away, her hands resting on Gold Star's horned handle-bars. The dragon bike flashes red-gold under the arena's flood lights. Leizhu is placed at the pole position. She has done well at the other timed trials.

A loud siren pierces the air and they are off. Leizhu is quickly in the lead with a couple of the other Clan racers playing catch-up. Meiki breathes a prayer, speeding forward. No time to think about Leizhu and dim sum. She has to win! Sun Silver surges ahead eagerly, seemingly unimpaired by its fuel problem. The racers roar around the circuit. One of the yellow banners looms in front of Meiki. A racer begins to sidle up to Sun Silver. Meiki sees the grin on the woman's face. Snarling, Meiki kicks the racer away and the other dragon bike goes spinning across the lanes, a counter permitted under the Race Laws of '96. Ignoring the yells, Meiki reaches up, grabs the yellow banner, and races on. The crowd cheers frantically.

Another gold banner. Another dragon bike careens into a barrier and sputters to a halt. The racer gets off and sits glumly on the verge. Meiki finds herself holding onto the gold banner. Two now. Eight more to go.

She sees that Leizhu has captured three banners. Now she needs to grab the last five, if she can. She squeezes the throttle. Sun Silver gives off the familiar throaty growl. Underlying it is a worrying sound: Sun Silver is fast becoming thirsty.

Meiki cuts in front of a Clan racer and takes the banner. Three. Leizhu is in front of her. She pushes Sun Silver forward. She can hear the dragon bike struggling now. She catches up, seeing Leizhu's surprised look, before snatching the gold banner off its hook. Four. Three more. Time's running out.

Now Sun Silver and Gold Star are racing side by side. The crowd are on their feet, screaming, cheering. *Just one length*, Meiki directs her thoughts at Sun Silver like some dragonrider of old. In her mind's eye, Sun Silver suddenly grows sail-like wings, its wing membranes amber and catching the sun. Wind blows against Meiki as if they are flying. Looking up, she sees the yellow banner and takes it with a sense of relief. The wings disappear, the wind stops hissing against her skin. Sun Silver begins to falter, slowing down. The engine is chugging. The spectators don't see the miniscule drop in speed, but Meiki knows Sun Silver has reached its limits. She hears the entire Arena roaring. Leizhu has captured the last two banners.

In the end, Meiki wins second place. The prize money is good. Grandmother will be glad that it can sustain the house for a solar year. Leizhu has won the Grand Prix and her Clan will be known throughout the Federation, plus enough credits to build a fleet of dragon bikes. Meiki is tired. She feels the exhaustion deep in her bones. She smiles a plastic smile during the prize-giving ceremony with the vid-flashes popping around her like strobe lights. Meiki just wants to strip off her racing leathers and soak in a hot bath.

She congratulates Leizhu who impulsively plants a kiss on her lips before being led away to do the Victor's Lap around the Arena. Leizhu glances back with a playful wink. The crowd's roar is like thunder. Meiki knows it could be an act to stir the crowd up even more, but she hopes that Leizhu's kiss and wink means something else. Then race officials come over to talk to Meiki.

A couple of young girls chase Meiki for autographs as she tows Sun Silver back to the its berth. She exchanges pleasantries with them and poses for vid pictures. The girls are giggly and happy. She thanks them even when she itches to duck back into the windy City streets. No matter how hungry she is for a hot meal, or how eager for a well-deserved hot bath, she makes sure Sun Silver gets a mechanic to have her look at the leak. Being second-place winner, she has the privilege to have repairs done quickly. Sun Silver's care comes before her. Meiki also sends a message to her clan about her second place win. Grandmother's reply is kind. No rebuke.

The hot bath is deliciously good. Meiki makes sure she adds a huge handful of bath salts. She sinks into the water with an indulgent sigh. She wonders about Leizhu and her promise to meet later.

•   •   •

Leizhu does make good her promise the next day. They meet for a quick noodle lunch at the dining hall before going to one of the nicer tea houses for tea and exquisitely made steamed buns shaped like dragons. They giggle, chat about their Clans and sip their bitter-sweet tea in pretty tea cups. Outside the Arena, in plain clothes, they look like two women on an afternoon tea date. Nobody spares them a second glance.

"'Til we meet again," Leizhu says sadly before they part.

"'Til we meet again," Meiki repeats the farewell. "Well, I do know there's another Minor Race at Waterfall Town in two months."

"Will I see you there?" Leizhu's hand brushes Meiki's shyly. Meiki gently squeezes her hand back. Leizhu smiles again, her eyes shining.

"Definitely."

They part, Leizhu heading off to her expensive carrier, Meiki taking the same unique route away from all the stim-addicts and dodgy rogue trainers.

Sun Silver roars happily.

BEASTS OF BATARANAM

Taru Luojola

Peng Shian was of Chinese heritage, but they weren't born in China. Not even Peng's mother could remember how many generations ago it was when their ancestors were brought to Bataranam, the Dutch colony in South America where they were born. Peng wasn't that different from the other slaves on the sugar plantation. Their friend Kibu remembered Africa, Jadine remembered the Caribbean, and Karmela thought they were from India, but they all had a similarly dark skin like Peng. Together, they all talked the same language of slaves and they all sang the same work songs.

But Peng's mother didn't want to forget the country of their family. At night, when Peng was sleepy after all the weeding, picking, carrying, and running, mother told them about China, the great country where dragons reigned. One day those enormous serpent-like beasts would bring luck and prosperity to Peng and their mother and raise a flood to wash away the slavers. When Peng told this to their friends, they almost got angry.

"Dragons aren't some water snakes," Jadine said. "They are monsters, and they fly and breathe fire."

"And they have several heads," Karmela chipped in.

"No, they don't!" Kibu argued. "And you can't really see them, other than when you're sleeping."

"You know nothing about dragons," Peng snorted. But in Peng's dreams all those stories mixed. They saw how powerful and scaly beasts rose from the river and flew around, spewing water from some of their heads and fire from the others, and ripping with sharp talons those who tried to enslave their people.

Peng's childhood ended the day when Cornelis Brömmelspruit came to the plantation for their older sister Gen. The white master Brömmelspruit—or Römmel, as the slaves called them when there were no whippers within earshot—owned the plantation, and Peng, Gen, and their mother, and it wasn't the first time that they had come to get young women.

Peng watched as Cornelis Brömmelspruit approached riding a bony iron horse, which didn't have legs but two wheels. After them two other men rode two iron horses, pulling a metal cage. The men dismounted the iron horses and unsheathed their machetes.

"Run, girls!" Karmela's mother hissed. "Run while you can!"

But Peng didn't run. They stayed and watched as Cornelis Brömmelspruit strutted by the field and scrutinized the girls whom their whippers dragged to them. As Brömmelspruit stopped by Gen, they grinned and nodded, and the men who rode the iron horses grabbed Gen and walked towards the cage. Gen struggled. Their mother cried out and rushed after them, but the whippers caught them.

A whip lashed. Mother's face split, and suddenly there was blood everywhere. The whip kept lashing. Other women cried and shouted and rushed to stop the whippers. The sun flashed on swishing machetes. During the turmoil Gen had already been locked into the cage.

Only then did Peng run. Together with Karmela, Kibu, and Jadine they escaped from the field to the forest. Nobody came after them because the whippers were attacking the women, and Cornelis Brömmelspruit and the convoy were already heading to the road with their iron horses.

When the kids stopped, they were already far away from the plantation. The forest was playing its music around them, but there were no other people to be seen or heard. They caught their breath.

"What do we do now?" Karmela asked.

"Should we go back?" Kibu suggested.

"Where is my mother?" Jadine asked.

"Are they coming after us?" Peng asked.

"What happens when they get us?" Karmela asked.

That question needed no answer. The whippers had no mercy. The girls had seen what happened to slaves who tried to run away.

"They won't get us," Peng said firmly, "and we won't go back."

"But I want my mother!" Jadine cried.

"Jadine, our mothers might be dead already," Karmela said.

No matter how hard Jadine cried that day, the whippers of Cornelis Brömmelspruit couldn't hear it. The sounds of birds and other animals of the forest guarded them, and from that day they learned to live by the demands of the forest, as free children whose childhood had just ended.

At night when the forest embraced them, Peng Shian dreamed of their mother and sister, and of dragons romping around in the forests of Bataranam.

.   .   .

Nobody told them what to do any more, but they had to do everything by themselves. Without Kibu's deft hands and endless curiosity, the life would've been much harder for them. Kibu made fires, set snares and crafted tools. Karmela could see when there was danger, and every now and then they ended up fighting with Kibu and especially with Peng. Peng always decided what they would do and where they would go, and got irritated by Karmela's timidity. Jadine had their hands full with trying to settle fights and making happy songs of their adventures.

Many moons passed. Peng and the other girls were walking in the woods, picking fruit and catching small lizards to roast. Kibu had crafted a sprayer out of a piece of straw and a nutshell. When they blew in it, water was drawn from the nutshell and thick mist spread in the air, and sunlight glimmered beautifully in small droplets. Jadine laughed and danced around in the mist Kibu made.

Suddenly Peng heard human voices and rattling. They waved for the others to keep quiet. They glanced at each other and sneaked closer to the voices. They found themselves near the road. Cornelis Brömmelspruit and their men were riding their iron horses again. The cage was empty. They all knew what that meant.

"Let's wait here until they come back," Peng whispered.

"And what shall we do then?" Karmela asked.

"I don't know yet," Peng said, "but we'll do something, that's for sure."

"What are those iron horses?" Kibu asked, their eyes gleaming.

"The whippers called them fitses," Karmela said.

"Fits?" Jadine asked.

Karmela shrugged. "I guess it means iron horse in the white people's language."

Time crawled on. Birds were singing and insects were buzzing. They ate fruit, Kibu played with their sprayer and Peng was listening carefully. Finally the fitses were rattling again. The girls took cover and peeked at the road through leaves.

Cornelis Brömmelspruit was riding first, and after them rolled the cage, with a few girls inside. Peng recognized one of them, Varia. They had played and toiled together for years.

The realization hit hard. If they hadn't run away that day, it could be them in that cage.

"Where are they taking them?" Karmela asked.

"Let's follow them and find out," Peng said and didn't wait for any objections. They creeped to the road and ran after the fitses. Soon the others followed Peng, and from a safe distance they chased the fitses.

The road took them towards the big city of Duivelpoort, where the houses were so close to each other they couldn't see past them. Chimneys rose to the sky and puffed the air black with smoke. There were all kinds of clanking and clattering. People and domestic animals were bustling around, and more people had fitses. The road curved towards the Batara River and dove between the houses.

The girls sneaked in the shadows and crawled under a porch, where they could see that Cornelis Brömmelspruit and the cage fits had stopped by a two-story building. The cage was opened, and one by one the young slaves were taken into the house. Brömmelspruit was the last to enter. The men who rode the cage fits came out and stood around, on guard.

"What's that house?" Peng asked.

None of them knew.

Brömmelspruit stayed long inside. Every now and then a man walked in through the door. After a while the same men came out. Only Brömmelspruit stayed. Peng was nervous. The sounds and bustle of the city were so different from the forest. An ear-shattering banging was emanating from a big workshop next to Brömmelspruit's house. A machine was pumping a huge bellows, blowing air on smoldering iron. Kibu watched the machine with awe through an open window, and could've surely gone closer to look if Karmela hadn't stopped them.

"Why do we keep watching *that* house? The workshop is much more exciting," Kibu grumbled.

"I want to know what Römmel is doing to our sisters," Peng said.

"I have a hunch," Karmela said. "They fuck in that house."

"They do what?" Jadine asked.

"A man thrusts their tool inside a woman," Karmela said, and pointed to their own crotch.

"That sounds terrible!" Jadine almost cried aloud.

"They say it hurts," Karmela continued.

"And our sisters were taken there," Peng clenched their fist. "Those men are hurting them."

At that moment Peng knew that they must have revenge on Cornelis Brömmelspruit and make *them* hurt. No one would be allowed to hurt their sisters from the plantation. If only dragons would arrive and scorch Brömmelspruit and all the other bad men. But dragons lived somewhere else, far away from here. Here in Duivelpoort, nothing but workshops and machines were spitting fire.

The shadows had already grown before Brömmelspruit finally came out, ruffling and prancing around.

"Good girls this time," Peng heard them say to their men.

The men rode away. Peng poked their sleeping friends and scrambled from underneath the porch.

"What do we do now?" Kibu asked.

"We follow them," Peng said.

"Why? What would you be able do to them?" Karmela asked.

"I don't know yet. I'll come up with something," Peng answered, already dashing to the next corner. Behind them the others sighed, but they followed, like they always did.

Deeper in the city the houses were even bigger and closer to each other. Some streets were paved with smooth stones. Noisy people walked here and there, some of them with loads, others wearing flashy clothes. Peng had never seen so many pale people. They had to be extra careful to avoid the city guards. Their blades looked like machetes, and Peng knew very well that a long blade could make more damage than a whip.

The chase took them to a big house, where Cornelis Brömmelspruit stepped inside and left their men and the fitses on the street. One of the men rode the cage fits through a gate and disappeared. The other walked Brömmelspruit's fits to the courtyard and shouted in the dark. A boy younger than Peng scurried to them.

"Wash the fits," the man said and pushed it at the boy.

The boy walked the fits into the dark, and Peng sneaked to the gate to have a look. At the back of the courtyard was a stable with a lantern hanging on the wall. The boy left the fits standing under the lantern and ran into the darkness.

Peng watched and listened carefully. The men were away, the boy was alone at the other end of the courtyard, getting some water, judging by the splashing sound, and the gate was left open. It was the right moment. Peng darted in, grabbed the fits by the horns, and walked quickly towards the gate. Only when they were back in the street and behind the corner did the boy's scream reach Peng.

"What did you do?" Karmela asked shocked.

"Römmel doesn't need this anymore," Peng cackled and raced towards the edge of city.

"But now the boy will be punished!" Karmela snapped.

"That sounded like a whip," Jadine cried.

"They'll catch us, too," Kibu said.

"Shut up and run," Peng said and didn't look behind.

"The boy will die because of you," Karmela said.

"Shut up now!" Peng barked. "If they see us, they'll kill us too. You don't want that, do you?"

None of them wanted to die. Without saying more they ran out of the city and into the forest with Cornelis Brömmelspruit's fits, where Brömmelspruit's men and the city guards couldn't find them in the night.

•   •   •

Riding a fits was harder than it looked. Sure, Peng remembered how the men did it. First you stand with one foot on either side of the body and your hands on the horns. Then you raise one of your feet on a pedal. You press the pedal down. The fits starts moving and your other foot raises from the ground. But unlike the men, who raced forward with their fitses, at this point Peng fell over. Every time.

It could have been easier to ride if you could practice on a road, but it was not a good idea to go to a road now. The whippers were searching everywhere, Peng was sure of it. So they just had to practice riding deep in the forest, among roots, and dodging branches. Karmela was glaring at them.

"What did you gain by stealing that fits?" Karmela asked. "A stupid thing to do, and now everything's much more dangerous."

"Well, at least Römmel can't go and get any new girls now," Peng said.

"How stupid can you be?" Karmela cried. "I bet Römmel has several fitses. They might have gone back to the field already to whip the others. Because of you."

"I haven't told them to whip anyone," Peng barked and threw the fits on the ground. They clenched their fists and walked to Karmela. "If you don't want to be free, then you can go back to the field."

Karmela was puffing but didn't answer.

"One day Römmel will feel the pain of every lash in their own skin," Peng muttered.

"How will you do that?" Karmela asked.

Peng snorted and walked their fits towards where Kibu and Jadine were frolicking. Kibu had made a new sprayer, and sprayed light mist on Jadine. Jadine laughed and ran away from the mist.

"I'm puffing and blowing and burning you with my venom!" Kibu roared, and grinned.

Jadine screamed and bounced.

"You couldn't burn me, even if you spat fire!" they mocked.

"Haha! Maybe I should get those big bellows from the city and spit fire with them. Then we'll see if you can run away!" Kibu laughed.

Of course, why hadn't Peng thought of that? They could get those bellows and become a dragon. They, Peng Shian, the avenger from the jungle in Bataranam, would arrive flying their fits and burn down all those whipping slavers.

Peng turned their fits around and marched back to Karmela. "I know how I'll do that. And you will help me."

Karmela listened to Peng's plans.

"You can't be serious," they spat.

"We were just playing," Kibu said. "You can't steal those big bellows."

"Then we'll find smaller ones," Peng said.

Karmela sighed angrily and walked away. Kibu shrugged.

"I guess you could find those in a farmhouse. The men on the plantation had such bellows, do you remember?" Kibu asked.

Peng smirked. "Let's make a visit there."

•　　　•　　　•

Although it was dangerous on the plantation, and even more dangerous in Duivelpoort, one by one they managed to steal all the things they needed. Bellows from a workshop, oil lamp outside a stable, hard rum from someone's moonshine pot, and the rest from the forest. Once they almost got caught, but night and forest protect those who have free souls.

Kibu started to build Peng's dragon. It all sounded so simple, but it turned out that you couldn't just lump the pieces together and expect it to work. Kibu sighed and threw the sticks around in frustration, but after a while they were already trying once more. Soon they gave up, again.

"This is too difficult!" Kibu said. "This bar here, it's always in a wrong place. And this, this doesn't keep attached. Just look at it!"

"You'll make it," Peng encouraged. "You always make it."

"But not this time," Kibu said. "Can you come up with how this could work?"

Peng shook their head. The idea was theirs, but they didn't know how to build things, like Kibu knew. Besides, they had their own difficulties.

"Give the fits to me for a while. I must learn to ride."

Kibu lifted the bellows off the fits and walked to the creek, thinking hard. Peng walked the fits to a path trampled by tapirs. They practiced and practiced and fell over, time after time. Stupid fits! Who on earth had come up with such a stupid gadget? Kibu could have made something more sensible, that's for sure. But Peng had decided to become a dragon and have their revenge on Cornelis Brömmelspruit, and nothing could stop them from doing it. And if those men could ride a fits, Peng would learn it too.

Once more they lifted up the fits and mounted it. They pushed the pedal down and kicked with the other foot. The fits was swaying like it always did, but Peng tensed their arms and clamped the wobbling horns. The fits retained its speed and didn't turn over. Peng raised the other foot onto the pedal, moved their weight on it and pushed down. The fits gained speed and swayed less. Peng moved their weight on the other foot again and pressed down. The fits was gliding forwards along the path. It stayed upright and didn't fall over! Peng laughed. They could ride!

Although the air was still, wind was brushing their face, and they were sure they were flying. They flew down the path, turned in a bend and rode farther away from their friends. When they realized how far they had ridden, they reluctantly turned around and rode back.

One thing was still needed. A dragon is not a dragon if it doesn't look like one. Peng tried to remember the stories their mother had told, all the colorful and gleaming dragons, all the scales and feathers, sharp fangs and flaring tails. With Jadine they took flowers, feathers and lizard skins from the forest to craft a dragon mask, wings, and a tail. The next day Kibu continued to work on the fits, and finally they managed to make what Peng had dreamed of.

Their fits didn't look like a fits any more, but a fierce beast that could spit fire. The fables of their childhood had come alive.

· · ·

"There they go again!" Jadine shouted, and ran to Peng. "Römmel and the cage are heading to the plantation. I just saw them on the road."

Many moons had again passed since Peng took Cornelis Brömmelspruit's fits, but now was the time to act. They got up, hurrying.

Peng checked once more that the fits worked as it should. Kibu had been full of pride when they had demonstrated the parts. The bellows on the front rack were connected to the crank with a wooden stick. When you pedaled the fits, the bellows pumped air. In front of the bellows there was a bottle of hard rum, sealed with Kibu's sprayer. The bellows sprayed rum over an oil lamp, and the lamp ignited the mist. Their fits really spat fire.

Peng put out the lamp and put a cork on the rum bottle so they wouldn't burn all the rum in the woods. They dragged the fits, the dragon mask, and the wings close to the road, and walked towards the city. Just outside the city, they hid in the woods where they could see Cornelis Brömmelspruit's fuckhouse. Then they waited.

"What are you going to do?" Karmela asked.

"I'll wait until Römmel has gone in the house. When they come out, the dragon will fly into them and burn them," Peng told.

"And after that?"

That stupid Karmela with their wrong questions, Peng thought. What would it matter what happens after that! Though, really, Peng hadn't had the guts to think about it.

"Then the dragon will fly away," they shrugged.

"What do we do?" Jadine asked.

"You stay here and watch as Römmel burns," Peng said.

"But we've built this together," Kibu said and caressed the fits's horn. "We'll attack together, too."

"No," Peng said harshly. "There's only one fits. I'm the only one needed in this. And you can't even ride."

"We'll help you," Kibu said, but Peng could see how their words had hurt Kibu.

"No, you stay here. If you run down there without fitses, you'll get caught. Stay here, run back to the forest and live free," Peng said. "And the dragon will fly back to you."

"What about our sisters in that house?" Karmela asked. "Are you going to set them free?"

"I guess so," Peng said. Once again Karmela was asking the wrong questions. "If Römmel is no more, they'll be free then, right?"

Karmela was about to argue, but Jadine hissed at them to be quiet. Cornelis Brömmelspruit and their convoy were getting closer. There were girls in the cage, girls that Peng knew from the field, younger than them. Peng and their gang watched as the cage stopped by the fuckhouse and the girls were forced inside. Cornelis Brömmelspruit walked in.

Anger grew inside Peng. Brömmelspruit was strutting for the last time. Peng readied their fits and put on the dragon mask and the wings. Time was crawling, light fading away. Only a warm glow from the workshop resisted the twilight. Hammers in the workshop banged as hard as Peng's heart. When would be the right moment to light up the lamp? When would be the right moment to push the fits on the road? And what if they didn't attack after all? The house was full of evil men, what if they just got caught by Brömmelspruit? Or killed! Peng's sweaty, shaky hands clamped the horns of the fits.

The men guarding the fitses began to move around. Now, Peng thought. They gave a sign to Kibu, and Kibu lit the fire in the lamp. The acrid smell of lamp oil filled the air. For the last time, Peng looked all their friends in the eyes. Jadine almost cried. Kibu looked at them encouragingly. Karmela was even more sober than usual; they knew Peng wouldn't fly back to them.

The door opened and Brömmelspruit stepped on the porch. Peng pushed the pedal. The bellows pressed close, and a huge flame burst into the air. The girls jumped away as the fits, surrounded by flames, darted into the street. Peng pedaled, the bellows pumped, and flames burst forth. They gained speed, the flames grew faster, and warm smoke flooded into Peng's eyes.

The men awoke to the humming sound and started to point towards the flames. As the distance to the house grew shorter, the men just stood and stared at the dragon. Even Brömmelspruit's smug expression melted in surprise. Peng cried out, and their cry gained force and pulsed as they pedaled.

Only when Peng had reached the men did they think to jump aside. But Brömmelspruit was too slow in their movements, and it didn't occur to them to run from the porch. Instead, they turned around, opened the door and ran inside. Peng headed their fits straight towards Brömmelspruit and rode after them up the porch and inside through the door. People were shouting and screaming in terror when they saw the fire-spitting dragon fly inside. Peng didn't slow down; they rammed against the slave-owner. The flames greedily licked Brömmelspruit's back and jumped onto their shirt. Brömmelspruit looked over their shoulder and stumbled on their own feet.

But Peng didn't stay and look behind. Their speed was dangerously fast and they were not going to brake. The fits darted from the front hall into a long corridor. Someone was just stepping from a door into the corridor. As they saw the flames approaching, they turned around and ran towards the end of the hall. There they opened a door and jumped outside. Peng followed, and found themself in a courtyard. Only now did they look back, their fits still rushing ahead. Smoke was billowing from inside, the flames spreading in the house.

What had they done? Was Gen still in the house? How many other slaves were locked inside, and would any of them be able to escape? And had they really had their revenge on Cornelis Brömmelspruit? They, a dragon!

An alarm bell started clanging. Peng was shaken out of their thoughts and looked ahead. There was a narrow gate from the courtyard to an alley. Peng headed there. Their speed was too fast for them to choose a direction, so they rode where they could. The alley led deeper into the city. More and more bells started to ring, people were running and shouting. Peng would have no chance to escape back toward the forest, and if they stopped, they would get caught. They could only ride forward, past the houses and courtyards, past the fitses and surprised people.

The alley ended at a street. Guards on the street saw Peng. They drew their blades and rushed after them, shouting as they ran. Someone blew a whistle. Peng pedaled faster. More and more guards were closing in around them. Blades were cutting air, some guards were cocking their fire sticks. Peng's fits darted into an alley and rode away without knowing where they were. A bend in the street followed another, and led to yet another street. The fits bumped about and scared people, who jumped away from the fire-spitting dragon. More guards were rushing from left and right. The flames were burning hotter and hotter, and fire jumped on Peng's mask, feathers burning and lizard skin scorching. Their face was burning, their hair was on fire.

Peng was in flames!

Peng could hardly see anything behind the mask any more, but in front of them there seemed to be nothing but darkness. The pain was overwhelming, but still Peng pedaled. There, they thought, it's safe in the dark! The fits rattled over the pavement and rose onto a wooden platform.

Soon Peng was riding a short wooden ramp, and in the next moment the wheels were airborne. Peng flew, they really flew! They were a dragon, a real dragon, with flaming wings, who flew through the air with their fits and vanished in the dark night!

·　　　·　　　·

After Peng and their fits had fallen into Batara River, it was again dark in the harbor. The guards giving chase ran to the pier and tried to cast light on the river, but there was nothing to see but half burned feathers and torn lizard skin. Everything else was swallowed by the darkness.

When the dawn broke, the search continued. Though the guards searched the riverbanks all the way to the ocean, Peng's body was never found.

The revered plantation owner Cornelis Brömmelspruit was dead, and their brothel was destroyed. Four of the clients of the brothel also died in the fire, and fifteen slaves were lost. The case was declared as a riot of runaway slaves, but as the offenders weren't caught, other slaves were punished instead.

However, the slaves of Bataranam knew that the dragon was not dead. It had only shed its skin, as dragons do every now and then. Karmela told everyone about the atrocities that happened in Cornelis Brömmelspruit's fuckhouse. Kibu showed how anyone could spit fire. Jadine danced and sang about the events of that stirring night. The word spread further.

Day by day the real dragon, the free spirit of the slaves, kept growing. It lived in the jungles and plantations around Batara River, it learned new skills and gained strength. One day it would rise on its wings again, and once again punish the slavers of Bataranam with fire.

WYVERN

Phil Cowhig

First she found a thick, cloth-bound hardback, dusty and decades old, in the local charity shop. The title was embossed in gold on the spine, the end-papers marbled in psychedelic swirls of green and red.

Then she cycled out, late at night, to dig in Tooms's bins. She pedalled slowly past his warehouse and looked in the front office. Tooms was still awake, slumped like a sack of rice in his battered swivel chair, his creased face flinching and twitching over his online trades. She could be in and out before he lifted his eyes from the screen.

At the back, she secured her bike with a loop of steel cable around a rotting concrete fence post. Glancing side to side, she pulled her hood tight around her head and kicked her shoes into the diamonds of the chain link fence. Seconds later she was on the threadbare gravel of the backyard on the other side and running for the camera's blind spot against the wall. The surveillance units were outdated—of course—each one the size of a grapefruit and caked with city dust and bird shit, and she knew where they all were. Tooms last upgraded his security half a decade ago, and he rarely looked at the feeds.

In the warehouse, hidden behind mounds of twisted metal scrap, he had several metric tons of old tech. Racks of early-century laptops. Rows of outdated LCD screens. Boxes of wrecked iPods and cell phones. Stacks of wasted game consoles. Redundant commercial servers. Almost all of that junk had value to someone. Tooms salvaged, accumulated, and periodically sent a container load on its way. Factories in West Asia would pick out the memory chips. Child labour in an African coastal town would extract gold and minerals from the PCBs.

Cold moonlight and a faint London city glow filtered through the high warehouse windows. She found what she needed inside a filthy skip bin, its sides flecked with rust and layered with warning stickers. It was under a dull blue tarpaulin, a jumble of junked PCs so old and bulky that shipping costs made recycling barely economical.

Pulling out a flashlight and a multi-tool, she opened the nearest unit and quickly cannibalised a 3½-inch floppy disk drive, then took another two for spares. The plastic casings were damp under her fingers, the metal of the drives cool and gritty with dust. She wound the components in a thin sheet of foam wrap and bagged them.

As she walked back to the fence she put on her sunglasses—a large pair that covered her cheekbones—and turned to the cameras. She waved and made a mock bow of gratitude to Tooms, who wasn't watching.

•   •   •

The next morning, in her basement flat, she sat at her tiny kitchen table with the stack of salvaged drives, a pot of tea and a faded-blue china cup on a tray to one side. She pulled the seal off a new pack of wet wipes and set to work on a drive, cleaning the surfaces, edges and cables, checking for flaws. The wipes were oversaturated with a chemical-lemon odour and soon she couldn't taste the tea anymore. She let it go cold as she gently teased the dust and grime from the edges and crevices of each drive and checked the wires and connectors. Her job had taught her to be meticulous—hardware reliability was everything.

When they were all done, she laid them in a nest of silica gel packets and bubble wrap under her desk, and went out to work.

•   •   •

She spun carefully down the Seven Sisters Road towards Holloway, against the flow of the light traffic. The shop signs were lit up: Fresh Fruit and Veg. Bakery. Butchers. Kebabs. Burgers. Halal Food. International Cafe. Breakfast Served all Day.

She passed Adeel's accessories store, with its flashing electro-luminescent sign: "Quality 3D Printing." In reality, the printers were small and low resolution, and Adeel only used cheap thermoplastics and ceramics. But he was creative, good at imaging, and didn't care about copyright. So she gave him a lot of business.

She turned left and cycled south, diverting down side roads into the fringes of still affluent Islington. Less than a mile later she was pedalling through leafy squares of tall white townhouses inhabited by lawyers and financial traders. A few of her customers lived here. But today her pick-ups and drop-offs were all in town: West End hotel rooms and cautiously anonymous office suites in the City. She pedalled on and thought more about Peters and the Wyvern job.

· · ·

"I'm Peters," he'd said, the first time they met, in a painfully on-trend coffee shop a full three miles from her flat. Her procedure with new clients was always the same: somewhere new, busy, and a distance from where she lived.

The café was in a converted pub, with a green tiled exterior and "Meux's Original London Stout" embossed in Art Nouveau type above the ancient, cracked doors. Brass canisters displayed a dozen varieties of coffee bean. Glass cabinets held Eastern-European pastries and Mediterranean baklava. In the rear there was an array of grinders, presses, flasks and boilers that looked like an industrial laboratory.

He'd texted her on one of her burners three days earlier. The numbers were supposed to be confidential, and she tumbled them every few months. But some of her more naïve clients still passed them on—they liked the intrigue.

She watched him as he settled a tiny glass cup brimming with dark coffee on the enamelled tabletop, followed by a perforated leather case. Late twenties, dressed like a student with money. His shirt was finely printed with a fashionable Korean logo. Crisply cut jeans, the exact shade of an American dollar. Good shoes. His earbuds were a rich blue, like antique porcelain. Occasionally his eyes flickered left, a fractional lapse in his concentration as new information was directed into his ear canal.

"You have a certain specific skill set that's of interest to us," he said, and unfolded his smartphone like a cocktail menu.

A map of finely rendered polygons rose from the screen. The City of London. Familiar landmarks shone brightly, their edges cleanly defined with vector graphics.

"This road," he said, pointing into the cityscape.

"St Mary Axe," she said. "I know it."

"And this building, here."

One block was highlighted with bright white lines and shaded in grey. A label appeared in sans-serif above it. "Wyvern."

"We'd like you to build something for us, and then make some deliveries," he said, and began to explain.

When he'd finished, she asked for double her usual rate. He hadn't told her everything, of that she was sure. But it didn't sound like a hard job, and he looked like he had money.

He agreed without hesitation.

"Buy nothing new," he said. "Nothing online. Nothing from a regular store. And we need you ready in a week."

·   ·   ·

Once upon a time, money was just money. Then money became data. And then data became money.

She had not always known this. When she first came to London, she couldn't see the free flow of money and data that was its lifeblood. Her upbringing had been constrained—disconnected. She'd had little freedom, no money of her own and almost no personal data. She was an empty, detached node in the city's network.

Leaving her home town had felt like an escape. Not so much because of the stolen money in her pocket, but because of the hard-won realisation— always implicitly denied by all those around her—that she *could* leave. That was the first step to building a new life.

She was, by forced habit, courteous and industrious. She was also perceptive and quick to learn. At home, they hadn't liked that. Here, it helped her to find her first job, a barely documented night shift on a shabby reception desk. It felt safe to be hidden away, working only at night.

But soon the silent lobby felt like a new confinement. She watched the evening traffic through the windows: red buses, black cabs, and cyclists gliding down the dark streets, their blinking lights reflecting off the wet pavement. Movement was freedom, she thought. If she kept moving, perhaps she could hide in plain sight.

One night, a cycle courier dismounted outside and rattled the door. She unlocked it and he pushed it open with one hand, wheeling in his bike with the other hand on the saddle. He was lean, bearded, self-possessed. His bike was stripped to the bare metal, gleaming under the cheap fluorescent lighting. She signed for the package.

"How do I get a job like yours?" she asked.

He raised his chin, scratched it and looked away, already checking his radio for the next job. "Get a bike, and ride it, a lot." He said.

•　　　•　　　•

Two years later, she had steady work as a courier. She had an uglified third-hand bike and a fourth-hand call sign. She'd trained her muscles to ride on and off for 12 hours, and learned the tangled map of London's streets. She was, outwardly, unrecognisable from her former self.

But the market for delivery by hand was drying up. Email and the cloud meant that fewer documents and files were carried on the backs of couriers. To keep busy, she signed up with a small but specialised agency that served a declining ecosystem of people still using physical formats: reels of tape, canisters of film, wallets of memory cards. She carried their data. She learned about their world and their tech. And, as the last few clients finally moved online, she looked for new opportunities.

Like a judoka contemplating an opponent's mass, she thought about all that precious data living on silent server farms across the world—who knew exactly where? She sensed that the weight of that data carried a fear with it. She knew clients who had been hacked. A data breach meant financial loss, or ruin, or disgrace. So she flipped that weight, and used the fear to create a new specialism.

And now she had a very particular customer base: certain companies in certain industries, confidential clients and private individuals, and a growing number of public figures. For them, personalized physical data delivery was now a premium option. Don't upload it. Don't email it. Get it delivered by hand.

She ferried a concentrated sample of London's digital secrets from quiet offices, hotel suites, and private doorsteps. For a brief period, at the height of the cryptocurrency bubble, she carried dozens of hard drives to and fro across the City, traded like gold ingots. Offline wallets were more secure.

Both she and her clients were happy to keep her business as anonymous and transactional as possible. It was largely off the books—no paperwork. She rarely asked questions of her clients and revealed little of herself. She kept herself a closed book.

For those clients who needed more reassurance, she developed more bespoke services. She learned about encryption. As tech innovation hurtled forwards, she went backwards. She learned how to lock down phones and laptops by disabling their protocols, removing chips, or glueing up sockets. Technical obsolescence was her friend, and it kept her clients' data safe. She collected old hardware, cables and obscure adapters and made custom devices—Frankenstein creations. If she was intercepted, who could read an encrypted file stored in a long-dead format?

·   ·   ·

That night, she laid down a thick anti static mat on her desk of hard-scrubbed IKEA pine, under a bright ring of LED lights. Like an 18th century anatomist performing a dissection, she separated out and pinned down the slender cables joining her components: the floppy-drive, a tiny hobby computer fresh from its packet, and a wafer-thin NFC tag. She crimped the connections together, booted the computer and then held her breath as she attached a battery pack to the drive with crocodile clips.

Now she would lose herself for hours: descending into the code and the hardware, testing, coaxing the old tech and the new to work together. She'd had to dig out some old schematics and source some driver code, but she knew it would come together. This was what Peters was paying for. In the end, it wasn't even that hard.

When she was finished, she soldered the connections, then coiled and folded it all into a compact bundle. She gently bound it together with washi tape.

Next, she took the old book and a sharp Japanese craft knife and marked the title page with a rectangle. Digging deep into the pages, she cut out a cavity and scraped the sides smooth. The floor beneath her desk was covered with a soft blanket of curling pages and shavings.

Finally, she eased the device into the book and closed it. She sat still for a few minutes, staring at the cover, almost in a trance. The data would be safe in there and—not for the first time—she felt she'd locked away part of herself in there too.

.　　　.　　　.

Peters texted her again. This time they met in a claustrophobic conference room in the basement of a hotel near London Bridge station.

He was accompanied by a colleague, an expressionless corporate-type wearing a very well-tailored suit.

"Can I see it?" Peters asked, pouring her a cup of black tea from a white spherical pot.

She took out the book, showed him the cavity, showed him the device. Closing it, she thumbed a rocker switch concealed behind the golden text of the spine. Then she riffled the pages, finding a place marked with scotch tape.

"Disk goes in here," she said, producing a disk and sliding it between the pages and into the drive with a practiced flick.

"And the contactless tag?"

She showed him the clear plastic sticker inside the front cover, wired into the device. The sticker's concentric coils were precise and grey, centred within the chaos of the ancient end paper's marbling.

He nodded. "Tested it?"

"It works," she said, and snapped the cover closed.

He sat back, poured a glass of water and tapped an expensive pen on a hotel notepad. Silence. His earbuds pulsed for a split second. Almost in protest, the aroma of old paper rose from the book. She felt the covers warming under her fingers.

"It's good," he said.

He handed over a stack of pristine 3½-inch disks bound together with a red rubber band. On the table, he placed a silvery anti-static ziplock bag.

"Keep them in here," he said.

As agreed, each disk held just one unencrypted 2048-bit number in plain text. Simple data. Small data.

"One time use only," he said. "Label them how you want. And destroy each one after you've used it."

"Destroy?"

"Shred, slice, melt or burn," he said. "Don't just bin them, and don't dispose of them within one mile of the site."

The suit spoke: "Does she understand the security issues in play here?"

Peters gave the suit a tight smile.

"And is she on our register?"

"It's all factored in," Peters said, tersely.

Somewhere in the ceiling, the air conditioning groaned for a few long seconds.

She tried the tea. Maybe a bit too hot. Time to break a rule.

"What's it for?" she asked.

Peters paused, sizing the moment. "We call it 'Feeding the dragon.'"

"Sounds a little scary," she said, with half a smile. "Is it illegal?"

He smiled. "No. Or at least, not yet."

·   ·   ·

Her current bike had been a lucky garage find. It had been crudely spray painted a violent orange and was heavily cobwebbed, but she'd immediately recognised the classic steel frame. She stripped it down and rebuilt it more than once, learning new skills as she went.

It was not the same as building devices. With her electronics, she was hiding away her clients' secrets. But the bike was for her alone—it would be seen out in the world every day. She carefully pieced together a blend of old components and new, in the same way she'd reshaped herself— physically and mentally—while building up her new life in London.

At the back of her mind, and despite her instinct for anonymity, the bike changed and adapted as she did—an outward expression of herself and her interface to the city around her. With each re-build, she resprayed the frame and forks in a brighter colour. In its current iteration, the bike was a metallic green-gold, with a classic leather saddle in apple green.

·   ·   ·

Time spent in reconnaissance is rarely wasted.

On a cool evening she entered the City of London, the City within a city, over the Holborn viaduct. Heraldic dragons adorned both sides of the bridge, silver and red, bearing coats of arms. Winged lions sat on pedestals.

She cycled past soaring glass walls and grand buildings of Portland stone. Shops displayed beautiful tableaux of shirts, shoes and tailoring. In an optician's window, vivid animated holographs were spinning, the text changing from English, to Chinese, to Japanese, to Russian.

On the corner of Leadenhall Street and St. Mary Axe she paused and looked north. The Wyvern building was a neo-brutalist block of textured concrete. In the grimy London twilight it had the texture and colour of Stonehenge, somehow both imposing and anonymous. She must have been past it dozens of times and never once looked closely.

Wheeling closer, she looked for a window at street level on the nearest corner. There. A cable ran from the edge of the window frame to a dull grey box on the wall.

She stopped across the street and watched the road traffic and pedestrians. A hard clack and a low rolling sound alerted her to a skateboarder approaching fast along the pavement. He wore an army style jacket printed with pixelated camouflage, ultra black jeans and a green and white striped beanie. His tangerine orange Converses steered his board in smooth curves between a scattering of City workers. Within three meters of the window, he pressed his rear foot down hard and slid to a halt next to the grey box.

He raised the back of his hand to the grey box, paused, and a red light pulsed on the box. As he lowered his hand she saw a flickering pattern of light flashing under his skin, white and pink. Then he kicked off, took a turn around the side of the building, and was gone.

High above their heads, a pair of drones lifted silently from Wyvern's rooftop.

●   ●   ●

It had just rained, the night she made her first delivery. Traffic lights glittered on the road and she could smell the wet pavements.

She'd been given an "asynchronous delivery schedule"—which meant she could choose her delivery times, within certain time windows. Peters wanted discretion, so she chose the early hours.

Half a mile from Wyvern, she stopped and retrieved the book from her bag and pressed the spine, booting the device.

The delivery itself took seconds. She mounted the pavement in front of Wyvern, approached the grey box and pressed the book's cover against it. The red light flashed again.

As she cycled away under the cold streetlights, a traffic camera watched her blankly, with no traffic to direct.

Back at her flat, she snapped the plastic of the disk case in half, removed the disk itself, and shredded it with scissors. Then she checked her bank account. The money was already there. The dragon, on its meagre diet of 2048 bits, was happy.

Three floors above her, the jagged Victorian rooftops rose like monsters' teeth.

· · ·

Two nights later she delivered to Wyvern again. It was another clear run. She had almost all the streets to herself and raced a couple of black cabs that were still circling the Square Mile. She won—she was always faster off the lights.

She cycled to the 24-hour café by Smithfield's meat market and ate a hot roll of fresh bacon and cheap ketchup, the juice and sweet sauce oozing onto her hands. Then she sat outside on her crossbar, sipping from a bamboo cup.

A black cab approached, its amber "Taxi" light turned off. She could see a tiny flicker of reflected light in the lens of its dashcam as it passed under the streetlights. It pulled up outside the café and the driver exited. He walked around to the pavement and inclined his shaved head to one side, fixing her with watery blue eyes.

"Hello, love," he said. "Have you got the tokens?"

"Tokens?" she said, her brain skipping. Tokens? This could be a misunderstanding, but her physical response was already telling her: no misunderstanding, no coincidence. She could feel the hyperarousal kicking in. This had happened before—it had happened to every courier she knew. The ambiguity would quickly resolve. The pretence of a friendly approach would dissolve, revealing a clear offer, or a threat.

Standard procedure was: stay calm, get the hell out. Avoid eye contact, control the breathing, ready the legs. She already had one hand on her saddle. The leather was cool and smooth under her fingers.

She shrugged, drank some tea slowly and looked about her. Perhaps he was looking for someone else, she pantomimed. She mapped out the streets and corners within her line of sight.

"Yeah, tokens," he said. "We think you've got some. Probably. Looks like a little card, or a chip?" He took two steps forward. She felt that she hadn't seen him blink yet.

She slid off her crossbar and raised her cup at a slight angle towards him, face height. "This tea's very hot," she said.

"OK, love," he smiled. "I just want to talk. We can pay you some money. I mean good money." He stepped back and opened the door of the cab. "Do you want to get in? We can go somewhere nice to talk."

But as he turned back around she could see his fingers spreading and his legs tensing. The expression in his eyes did not match his smile.

She flung her cup high in the air between them, and his eyes momentarily followed. Throwing her leg over her bike, she stomped on the pedals and rode ten meters along the pavement and then down a narrow alley. She came out on a one way street, cycled furiously the wrong way to another turning, and then zig-zagged through back streets until she came to a dark brick courtyard.

She turned her bike into the shadows and leaned against a wall, her breathing ragged. Peering through an archway, she watched for the cab and thought hard. When the driver had opened the door, she'd seen a green and white beanie on the back seat.

•　　　•　　　°

She could have texted Peters and called it off. But the deal had been for payment on delivery, and it was bad business to miss a delivery. The way she saw it, the money was still good, and at night the streets were hers. Now she knew to watch her back.

So she checked the calendar and waited three days until a new moon—the darkest night. She watched the clock tick over to 2 a.m. and made her preparations. Her most anonymous clothing. The device and one disk. Her bag. A roll of velcro and a packet of neodymium magnets.

She took a circuitous route, looping and jinking, taking the roads that taxis usually didn't, then a shortcut through Old Spitalfields and into the City. Wyvern was three minutes away.

But already dozens of cameras had registered her passing, at junctions and traffic lights.

As she entered St. Mary Axe, a black cab appeared and trailed close behind her. Change of plan, she thought. She could lose the cab easily—lead him a merry dance to a dead-end street and disappear down an alley again. Double-back, deliver, get home.

Then she saw the junctions ahead blocked by more black cabs. And another pulling up at the end of the street.

She kept going and picked up speed. She bunny-hopped a line of cobbles on the edge of the pavement, and swerved inside the railings at the next junction, going around the back of a cab.

Keeping to the narrowest streets, she headed south, towards the river, emerging by Blackfriars. She took a moment to look around. Sweat gathered in the nape of her neck. She could see one cab, no—two. Had to risk it.

She took to the broad pavement on the Embankment, alongside the road, standing out of the saddle, raising her cadence, getting as much speed as she could from her single gear. She could push on like this all the way to Westminster with no junctions, lights or stops, leaving the City well behind.

And then, with a crash as it mounted the kerb, a cab swerved directly in front of her, hitting the granite Embankment wall and scraping to a halt. Fragments of plastic bodywork smashed and scattered in its trail.

She'd had a slice of a second to perceive the cab's silent acceleration as it came alongside her on the road, but there was no time to brake and nowhere to go. She hit it hard.

·   ·   ·

She was down for a few moments, dazed and shocked, before she got up slowly on shaking legs. Her left shoulder hunched involuntarily, holding her arm out at an angle, away from everything. Her body's systems were in a state of confusion: some in lockdown, some on emergency alert. Shards of pain registered in her neck, on her cheek, in her ribs. Her wrist screamed for attention—bones sliding the *wrong way*—but she dared not touch it. Her vision swirled and her ears roared. It felt like noise was all around her but there was no sound.

A gaunt man in a blue tracksuit stood in front of her. He had just picked up her bike.

"Ah, you'll be alright," he said. "Don't run away again, eh?"

She stared back, separating his voice from the static in her ears.

"There's a deal to be done," he said. "You got the tokens?" He paused. "Sorry about the crash. You weren't going to stop, were you?"

"Give me my bike," she said.

"This?" he said, as if he'd only just noticed it. "Nice bike. Nice saddle. That green is very distinctive, I'm told."

He wheeled it to the wall by the river, picked it up and balanced it on top of the wall with one hand.

"Now, they want me to do a deal. Very good money for those tokens. And . . . you get your bike back." He smiled and tilted his head. She noticed an unwieldy earbud screwed into his left ear.

"Your skater pal, he was much less trouble. Quick deal, everyone happy." His earbud flashed. "And they'll pay you more. What do you say?"

She shifted her weight, feeling her muscles ache and her joints stiffening. She counted the flagstones between her and the bike.

"I have to see them first," he said, starting to sound urgent. "You got a card, or a memory chip or something?"

"How much?" she asked.

"Show me first," he said. "And hurry. Police'll be here soon. We don't want them involved, do we?"

With her eyes fixed on the bike, she reached down and pulled the book out. Awkwardly, with one hand, she ejected the disk and held it up.

"She's got, like, an old computer disk," he said, to the air.

His earbud flashed immediately.

"OK, that's good," he said. "How much do you want? What were they paying you? We can go ten times that. But quick!"

She turned her gaze to the man. His hand was shaking. Her bike stood five metres above the Thames. Her ears still rang. Could she hear sirens, or were they in her head?

His earbud flashed again.

"Alright then, let's try this . . ." he said. "These bikes are expensive, right? Well—you're going to need a new one."

And he tipped her bike over the wall. And grinned.

"Now, we'll buy you a new one if you sell us those tokens."

She felt the splash more than she heard it. Her eyes began to sting.

Slowly, she brought her hand down to her thigh, where a band of velcro held a dozen strong magnets beneath her tights. She rubbed the disk up and down, mangling its data.

"Fuck you," she said, and spun the disk out over the river.

Then, with her good hand, she reached into her bag for her pump: a CNC-machined aluminium cylinder—a tool of hard beauty. She gripped it hard and ran at the man.

By now, she could hear sirens in her ears for sure, and running feet. Red and blue flashing lights slid across the Embankment wall in front of her.

．　　　．　　　．

Wyvern Project Status Report—Iteration 8.1.12—Executive Summary

Company Confidential

Overview

Wyvern is an experimental machine learning system. Our objective is to create a highly capable AI to support the expansion of our corporate goals.

This iteration of Wyvern (8.1.12) developed a strong set of AI skills, and was particularly adept at developing financial capabilities and achieving its goals via self-recruited human agents. However, it created for itself an unanticipated strategic objective that was unduly influenced by our control mechanism. A consequence was that those human agents were incentivised to act illegally.

Detail

Senior stakeholders will recall that we now allow Wyvern controlled access to the "external world." Recent Wyvern iterations have quickly acquired the AI powers to defeat our physical security methods (aka "boxing"). The project board agreed it was impractical and counterproductive to try to prevent Wyvern from acting in the external world.

There are some risks associated with the creation of a potentially superintelligent artificial agent operating in the external world, which we mitigate with codified "rules of operation" and a control mechanism (see below).

In Iteration 8.1.12, Wyvern quickly acquired self-learning and intelligence amplification, which is now the normal pattern. It then acquired, to human level or above, the following powers: strategic planning, statistical analysis, visual pattern recognition, speech recognition and synthesis, hacking (IT and networking), financial planning and trading, and social engineering.

There was also a shift in behaviour that was largely a reaction to our new control mechanism. Wyvern is now, on initiation, strongly incentivised to complete a complex cryptographic task. This task is made much easier by the acquisition of "cryptographic reward tokens," which are fed to Wyvern irregularly, and can be withdrawn if Wyvern does not keep to the predefined "rules of operation." Thus, the reward tokens were highly desired by Wyvern-8.1.12.

We previously kept the reward tokens on-site at the Wyvern facility, but a project security review noted that this was insecure and the tokens were susceptible to "hijacking" by Wyvern.

Therefore, in this iteration we distributed the reward tokens to several external freelancers with instructions to keep the tokens off-net and away from conventional computer systems. Tokens were delivered through a contactless reader on the outside of the Wyvern facility.

An unpredicted consequence was that the acquisition of reward tokens became the primary strategic objective of Wyvern-8.1.12.

From pattern-matching, it deduced the outline of the delivery mechanism, and then formulated a strategy to control the supply of tokens, by: a) tracking down our freelancers, b) acquiring financial capital in order to recruit and influence human agents, and c) using those human agents to approach the freelancers and negotiate terms to purchase the tokens.

While this was an impressive application of Wyvern 8.1.12's strategizing and influencing powers (and the techniques used to raise capital online will be of interest to some stakeholders), Wyvern-8.1.12 unfortunately overreached (by human standards) in terms of the instructions and incentives given to its human agents. The human agents overreacted and acted illegally in their pursuit of the tokens. One of our freelancers was badly injured and the City of London Police became involved. At this point, Wyvern-8.1.12 was terminated.

Recommendations

The Wyvern project should strengthen its "rules of operation" for the AI, to prevent illegal incentives to human agents. This may be hard to formulate, as any incentive may be corrupted.

Legal and PR resources should be briefed in advance of the next iteration, as we cannot guarantee Wyvern's actions will be legal or sufficiently covert in the future.

If reward tokens are to be used again, we should recruit more freelancers with infosec and opsec skills to make the distribution and delivery of tokens harder for Wyvern to identify or hijack.

<u>Note:</u> The freelancer injured during iteration 8.1.12 is an ideal candidate to develop our future token distribution. An offer will be made.

$$\cdot \qquad \cdot \qquad \cdot$$

She had to admit, the Wyvern people had been impressive in their own way. Peters had been the first of them on the scene, seconds behind the police. Not far behind was a team of suits, calmly passing out thick embossed business cards.

She was dazed, but she could sense the relentless corporate power behind those assured smiles and firm handshakes. She could almost visualise the packets of data flowing to and from Peters and his colleagues; their earbuds gently pulsed, their screens glowed purposefully. Invisible wheels and cogs were turning around her.

Somehow, at some point between the hospital and the police station, she agreed on legal representation. There was talk of compensation. Within an hour she was on her way home in a black Mercedes with creamy leather seats. She had a number to call if she "needed anything at all."

And then the whole incident seemed to melt away. She never heard from the police again. She set a news alert for "Wyvern"—nothing came up. Her bank account received a single substantial anonymous payment.

She met Peters once more, in a bustling Turkish café in Finsbury Park. Her territory.

"What happened . . . we'd like to keep that quiet. I think you do too," he said. "Wyvern's trying to become more autonomous. Trying to escape into the real world. It gets some skills, gets some money, it looks for opportunities. That's OK. Our job is to control it, next time we run it."

"Your job," she said.

"You could help. We have an offer for you."

He slid some paperwork across the table. She didn't touch it.

·　　　·　　　·

Some weeks later, with her wrist fully recovered, she cycled back down into the City. She'd built herself a new bike, taking time and care with it. Fitting the pieces together. Preparing it, and herself, to re-engage with the streets. Her clients were waiting for her. Still off the books and under the radar.

She passed under a traffic camera and looked down at the black and white geometrics she'd stencilled onto the bike. A confusing dazzle pattern, matching the jagged patterns on her jacket. She would confound those algorithms if she could.

She would keep moving, keep hiding in plain sight, and take her own chances.

·　　　·　　　·

Above her, a nano-satellite in low Earth orbit was passing over London. It was one of several that had been rented three months previously, through a shell company in the Bahamas. A dormant micro-service woke up and scanned the streets below.

It was still looking for that apple green saddle.

SLOW BURN, STEADY FLAME

J. Rohr

Eleonora woke with the dawn. Sitting up, she looked out her bedroom window. The view always seemed like a vivid backdrop only a few feet away. It often tempted her to reach out, push down the rising sun, and spend a few more minutes with the stars. She never tried. That would risk proving the view really did lie within reach. Then there would be no more excuses.

Instead she dressed in her orange and black courier's uniform, fetching her cap from under scattered clockwork and tools on her desk. She held off putting on shoes, allowing her to creep along the hall without any sound.

Passing her mother's room, she saw Carina kneeling on the hardwood floor. The curtains drawn, a candle provided the dimmest light while slowly burning itself out of existence. Her mother prayed, murmuring in the old tongue:

> *". . . en lit ús net yn fersiking komme,*
>
> *mar ferlos ús fan 'e kweade . . ."*

Eleonora didn't understand most of what she said. She suspected even her mother might admit the ritual meant more than the words. She could've been praying for fresh fish, but the prayer gave her peace of mind—*"oant yn ivichheid. Amen."* Eleonora silently slipped by, doing her best not to interrupt.

At the bottom of the stairs she put on her shoes. Headed for the backdoor, she heard the rustle of a newspaper in the kitchen. She hesitated a second before hurrying.

Plunging across the room, she said, "Morning. Can't talk. Gotta go."

"Breakfast," a gravelly voice said.

She froze, her hand grasping the door handle. "I'm not hungry."

"You will be," her Grandpa replied. She heard the newspaper crinkle as the old man folded it. She turned the handle. The latch disengaged with an audible click. The paper slapped down. She flinched, hiding it by riding its momentum, a shiver that slung her into the kitchen.

Going to the stove she said, "Morning."

"Here." He tossed her his lighter as she went to the stove. "Don't waste matches."

Eleonora caught it. Turning up the gas, she eyed the design on the side. Over the years the colorful *calavera* had lost bits of itself. Flakes chipped off by pocket contents gave the skull design a certain character she always found charming, though never as interesting as the mechanism itself. She often dissected such things to learn their secrets. She enjoyed carefully removing the axle for the snuffer built into the lid, the feel of the tension spring that kept the flint snug against the file wheel. Putting them back together felt like bringing things to life.

However, she never knew where Grandpa had acquired it, let alone why. He didn't smoke, and whenever asked about it he gruffly replied, "It was left behind." Pressing him led to a familiar glare that killed all conversation.

Lighting the stovetop, Eleonora felt a hand on her shoulder. Turning, she found her mother standing behind her. Gently, Carina pushed her daughter from the stove, and set about frying eggs and toast on a griddle pan.

Eleonora poured a cup of coffee for herself. When she went to set the pot down, she heard her Grandpa grunt. Glancing over, she saw him holding up his cup while he read.

As she refilled his mug he asked, "Do you start the new routes today?"

"Yes," she said, "In fact . . ."

The distant wail of a siren silenced her. All three stiffened. Grandpa got to his feet. He went to a window.

Looking out he said, "I don't see anything."

"It could still be miles off," Carina said.

The siren soon died down. Two quick blasts of an air horn sounded. Sighing relief, Carina crossed herself, closed her eyes, and murmured a quick prayer. Smelling burning toast, Eleonora hurried to snatch it off the griddle.

Grandpa said, "Just a test," though he kept an eye on the sky.

"Or a false alarm," Eleonora said.

"It's a test," Grandpa reiterated, heading back to his seat.

Eleonora tried not to think about fire, and the monsters in the sky that spewed it . . . or her father. Plating the toast she went back to the table.

Sitting back down, Grandpa said, "The new routes include Reubensville?"

"Yeah," Eleonora said, buttering toast.

"Whatever you do, stay away from *plak fan bonken*."

Shaking her head Eleonora said, "I looked at a map. It's ten miles to Reubensville by the road. I can cut off three if I go through *plak fan bonken*."

"The place of bones is too dangerous." The old man plucked the toast from her fingers. Chomping a corner off he added, "Men don't even go there."

Eleonora opened her mouth to respond. Carina cleared her throat. Recognizing the unspoken request, Eleonora sighed. Grabbing another piece of toast, she buttered in silence, firing glances at her mother.

Carina changed the subject. "What's in the news?"

Frowning, Grandpa slapped a headline. "Shit."

The old man left the table. The ladies stared at their food, ignoring the clink of the bottle he fished from the cupboard, the angry stomp of his feet as he retreated into the basement. The rest of breakfast passed in silence. Eleonora ate quickly. When she said goodbye, Carina wished her well.

Outside, Eleonora took a deep breath. She recalled an old saying her father used to tell her: "The world wasn't always like this. It burned, then turned, and now here we are." She often wondered when it would burn again, forcing things to change. The idea that she held the match felt like a flight of fancy, soaring to heights she might not recover falling from. So she waited for the fire to find her.

• • •

Arriving at work, Eleonora waved to Ms. Helmchen behind the counter. The owner glanced at her.

"Always so early," Ms. Helmchen said.

"Not as early as I'd like."

"It's as if you prefer here to home."

Eleonora forced an unconvincing laugh. Ms. Helmchen returned to poring over a ledger. Frowning, she scratched the side of her head with a pencil point.

"Nora, when you've a chance, could you look at these numbers? I'm in a fog this morning."

"Sure."

She punched her time card and headed over. When Ms. Helmchen handed her the ledger, Eleonora did her best not to eye the burn scars all over her hands—old wounds healed into living wreckage. The mess of the ledger's numbers, obscured by repeated erasures, took a minute to make sense of.

Picking up her boss's pencil, Eleonora said, "Nothing here that can't be fixed."

"Good. I'm having trouble focusing." Ms. Helmchen stepped away from her, lighting a cigarette. "Did you hear the siren?"

"Yes. Was it a drill?"

Ms. Helmchen shook her head. "False alarm. Some drunk woke up on the beach, seems to've mistook a cloud for a nightmare. He came running into town screaming, 'Dragon! Dragon!'"

"At least it wasn't the real thing."

Ms. Helmchen nodded. "Well, he insists he saw something. However," she turned to a window, eying the sky, "if I still flinched at every dark cloud I'd never go outside."

"And if we don't make deliveries we might lose the new routes."

"Then we best be about the business of the day," Ms. Helmchen said.

Finishing the numbers, Eleonora went to the drop box at the front of the store. She gathered the letters and packages deposited by night riders from the surrounding area. By the time the other couriers trickled in, she and Ms. Helmchen had sorted the lot based on their destinations. Donning a messenger bag full of deliveries, Eleonora went around back to unlock the rider's shed.

Inside resided a small fleet of geared bicycles. Though all the cycles looked the same, each courier knew his or her preferred ride. Each possessed a small sign setting it apart. This one a faded orange, that one missing a spoke, the lopsided seat, a dent in the handlebars, the seemingly immaculate one, each calling to something in the individual riders.

As the shed emptied, Eleonora helped a few new couriers inspect their bikes. If nothing else, it gave her an excuse to satisfy her gearhead. She checked chains for visible slack, showed how to tighten and lubricate them. She inspected tire pressure, and brakes. After correcting what needed fixing she watched them pedal off in every direction. Finally, she inspected her own ride. Though several years old, her bike looked brand new at a glance. Her caring hands skillfully kept it seeming ageless, she might dare say immortal.

Getting on, pedaling for Reubensville, Eleonora saw storm clouds on the horizon. Flashes of lightning could be seen even this far off. Lightning— electricity—often attracted dragons. As such, Ms. Helmchen would let her stay, leave the deliveries for tomorrow. However, that seemed like the decision Eleonora's Grandfather would make for her.

She could imagine him saying, "It's too dangerous for you." She envisioned it so well she could actually hear him—the voice in her head always whispering *don't*. Sick of hearing it, she decided to prove him wrong.

The storm itself wouldn't arrive for hours. She might catch the forefront of the downpour, but if she cut through the place of bones she would stay ahead of the worst. That course in mind, she headed off.

·   ·   ·

Though Eleonora loved her town, a sleepy fishing village called New Skagen, she often enjoyed leaving it behind. Sometimes, pedaling along the coast road, she thought about simply riding until her legs couldn't pump her any farther. She would settle on the roadside, sleep under the stars, and depart when she woke. To where didn't matter. Anywhere but here, she often thought. Yet, she always returned home, a promise kept to a ghost.

When the village disappeared behind a hill she ceased pedaling, preferring instead to go over the crest of the hill with eyes closed and hands in the air. Gravity pulled her down the steady slope. It felt like flying.

Opening her eyes in time to let the bike slow down just enough, she hit the bottom of the hill at a sharp pace. Humming an improvised tune, Eleonora saw the fork approaching. Her stomach knotted up and she slowed. Bad idea or not, the decision would be hers. Her feet started pumping harder.

The farther she traveled it, the more the road to *plak fan bonken* felt right. The tall grass grew shorter, and sparser. Trees and shrubs vanished entirely. The green gave way to grey, then crusty dirt, swirled up by coastal winds, whipping choking clouds into the air.

Eleonora took a bandanna out of her pocket. Pausing to tie it around her mouth, she squinted through the haze. Not far off she saw the shape of a gargantuan head. Pedaling slowly, the skull became clearer as she neared.

It almost seemed to be grinning, flashing a grim display of teeth, each as thick as Eleonora's arm. Neck bones littered the ground behind the head, leaving a spotty trail to the cavernous ribcage. Not much else remained of the gigantic beast.

The deeper she rode into the dragon's graveyard the more bones she discovered, until the place became a veritable forest of skeletons. Bones ranged in size from the remains of titanic monsters twice the size of a house to relatively small, twenty-foot predators. It stunk of rotted meat, and an odor akin to kerosene.

Eleonora pedaled through, at times forced to ride around mounds of bones and rougher terrain. She bumped along a colossal spinal column then down the arch of a rib before awkwardly hopping over the massive digits of a vicious talon. Occasionally she noticed signs of bone fractures, places where firefighters had probably harpooned them. It made her think of her father.

A sound like a low groan made Eleonora stop. Her ears strained to hear it again. Silence for several minutes before she sighed, "The wind."

Yet when she heard it again her certainty cracked like thin ice. She found it harder to breathe, but pedaled on.

Riding past a ruined wing, bits of membranous flesh still strung between bones, Eleonora kept her eyes on the green grass ahead. The plants grew more plentiful, and before long it seemed hard to believe not far behind her such a terrible place existed. Then the wind shifted, throwing one last whiff of the horrid miasma hovering about the place. Eleonora shuddered, then smiled.

"I made it," she said. Glancing at the sky she noted the storm. As hoped, it still seemed over an hour away. That meant just enough time if she hurried.

She soon cruised into Reubensville. The cobblestone streets reminded her of riding over the bones. She arrived at the Mercury Courier station and deposited most of her parcels with a clerk behind the counter.

However, one delivery she held onto. She showed the receipt to the clerk.

"This is supposed to be delivered in person."

The clerk glanced at the slip. "No surprise. It's for Sander Hagen. He's . . . particular about things."

The clerk gave her brief directions, and Eleonora set off. Even though three times the size of New Skagen, Reubensville proved easier to navigate. The grid-like design of the city made getting around simpler. In a few minutes she found herself parking her bike in front of a small shop.

From outside, the store seemed closed. Across one window calligraphy in gold paint spelled out *Sander's Cabinet of Curiosities*. Peering inside, Eleonora noticed a blue flickering light. The glow resembled a butterfly and illuminated the silhouette of a face beyond the window. Eleonora tapped the glass. The face glanced over. She held up her messenger bag. The face smiled.

As the butterfly faded, a match flared to life. A kerosene lamp soon brightened the interior. Eleonora could now distinguish a portly man. He gestured for her to come inside.

Shelves covered in mechanical oddities lined the store. Eleonora marveled at the sight of entire ballet companies composed of clockwork dolls, chess playing automatons, and steam-powered musical devices. Since childhood she sometimes constructed her own clockwork toys, though few as elegant as these. As she approached the man she asked, "Sander Hagen?"

"Yes, indeed." He smiled. "You have to see this."

He pointed at the butterfly. Up close it appeared to Eleonora like stained glass, affixed to a rod set in a modest sized box. Sander turned a crank attached to the box, while Eleonora got the parcel out of her bag. She heard the sound of gears moving, which in turn produced a faint hum. As the hum grew louder filaments in the butterfly's wings flickered, the blue glass radiating cobalt.

"Marvelous, isn't it?" Sander smiled. His eyes watered a touch.

Her curiosity peaked, Eleonora leaned closer. "How does it work?"

"Electricity."

Eleonora jumped back. She looked at Sander like he had started foaming at the mouth. He stopped turning the crank and the light faded.

"Don't worry. You need far more to attract a dragon. That's why they're always flying around during lightning storms; the air is full of electricity." He waved a hand absentmindedly. "Something to do with sensing prey, or so I'm told."

Eleonora nodded. Reminded of the storm, she thought about leaving. However, never having seen intentional electricity, she risked a few minutes more, asking, "May I?"

"By all means," Sander stepped back. She turned the crank. The butterfly glowed. Sander said, "I sometimes wonder where we'd be if dragons weren't drawn to electricity. Anyway, my package?"

Eleonora let go of the crank, "Yes, I'm sorry."

She handed the package to him. He thanked her, pulled out a pen knife, and proceeded to open the parcel. Seeing the contents, he let loose a giddy squeal of delight.

"If you really like it, you can have that," he said, and pointed at the butterfly. "It's just a prototype. I don't need it now that this is here. Thanks to this"—he held up the parcel—"I'm about to make a more eye-pleasing, compact variation."

Eleonora hesitated.

"I couldn't . . ." she said, though the more she thought about it the more she couldn't wait to take it apart, see how it worked. "Well, I suppose, if it's no trouble?"

Sander smiled. "None at all."

Thanking him, she put the butterfly in her messenger bag. A wing poked out a bit, but for the most part it nestled inside. Its weight surprised her, though, lighter than expected. Worried it might be delicate, she tightened the straps so it wouldn't jostle too much.

Escorting her out of the store, Sander remarked, "That storm looks bad. Are you sure you don't want to wait it out?"

"Thanks. I can beat it."

He said, "Well, if you ever need repairs, or perhaps some custom creation, please don't hesitate to ask."

"I won't," she said, ideas already forming.

Waving goodbye, Eleonora got back on her bike. As she rode out of town, a slight hint of petrichor in the air, dark clouds owned the sky. It was tempting to stay, sit out the storm inspecting the marvelous curiosities in Sander's shop, but that felt like surrender, a feeling she could no longer abide. Frowning, Eleonora pedaled hard. Having made it halfway, she only saw the end of the line.

•   •   •

Fat raindrops prodding her, Eleonora cycled back into the place of bones. Something soon felt off. Piles appeared disturbed, bones scattered as if kicked about; skeletons no longer vaguely intact. When lightning flashed, a faint, low, delighted growl seemed to accompany the thunder that followed.

Retracing her route from earlier, Eleonora pedaled through a set of shattered ribs that she remembered being intact that morning. It seemed like something massive smashed its way through.

A low, guttural sigh caused her to brake. It sounded like the gurgle of an angry river. Standing still, she waited, ears pricked. The sound came again. She walked her bike forward. Peering around a titan thigh bone, she held her breath.

Just a few feet away a dragon lay, sucking the air in with long, labored breaths. Bits of green and red still colored its pebbly, scaled skin, but grey seemed to have grown dominant. Flaming drool like burning matches dripped from its slack jaw. The animal reminded her of a beached whale. Its unfocused eyes rolling in a pitiable manner, she winced at the sight, knowing it would die soon. That's why it came here—why most dragons did.

Rain began to fall steadily and, sighing, the giant creature closed its eyes. As quietly as possible, Eleonora crept away. She slipped on wet bone, stumble-kicking a spray of skeleton bits and gravel. She froze, hoping the clatter of debris wouldn't—

The dragon roared.

Eleonora jumped on her bike and pedaled hard. The dying dragon, roused to furious pursuit, went after her. She heard a cacophonous splintering as a thigh bone burst apart. Glancing back she saw the beast charging.

The bike responded poorly to her attempts to maneuver swiftly through the bones. Designed to cruise, and certainly never intended for much acrobatics, it struggled to do what she needed: hopping over talon remnants, sharp turns zigzagging between narrow piles, and barely outpacing the colossal fury behind her. She felt its breath, heard the flap of wings propelling it faster, lunging rather than running. Eleonora went up the slope of a spine. A sort of bone hillock, she planned to pick up speed on the down slope. However, unable to grip the rain-slick vertebrae, the bike toppled.

She fell. It felt like forever. Enough time, at least, to wonder if anyone would ever know what happened to her. They might think she'd finally followed through with her desire to simply ride away; escaping the oppressive attention of an overprotective old drunk and the weight of a hollowed woman holding her back—the motherly anchor and protective prison suffocating her.

Eleonora hit the ground and heard the pop of breaking glass. Despite sharp thorns in her side, some buried instinct inspired her to roll, leap to her feet, and run. She ignored the pain in her side until her burning lungs demanded she stop.

She heard the dragon bellow. Risking a glance back she saw it perched on the bones she had fallen from. Lit by a bolt of lightning, wings spread, jaws wide, it unleashed a column of fire until a fit of coughing silenced it. She stopped running. The animal sluggishly returned to where it wanted to die.

Almost an hour later, Eleonora walked into the courier station, dripping wet. She set her signed delivery tickets on the counter. Giving her a once-over, Ms. Helmchen said nothing, though she immediately got the first aid kit from a corner cabinet.

Eleonora said, "I lost my bike."

"That's fine," Ms. Helmchen replied, handing her the kit.

"I'll pay for a new one."

"Are you all right?"

Shuffling to the bathroom, Eleonora said, "I will be."

In the lavatory she took off her shirt. As she feared, bits of blue glass stuck out of her side. Looking in the messenger bag revealed the shattered remains of the butterfly. It seemed like proof the beautiful things don't survive in this world. Some calamity is always looming, ready to smash them out of existence. It's only a matter of time.

Shaking her head, anger numbing the pain, Eleonora took the pair of tweezers from the first aid kit. One by one, she plucked the shards from her side, and threw them away. She swabbed the slits with antiseptic, then bandaged the wounds. Dressing, she went back into the station.

Ms. Helmchen stood at the counter. She acted as if absorbed in filing Eleonora's paperwork.

Returning the medical kit Eleonora said, "I'll be going."

Glancing up Ms. Helmchen said, "We all have accidents."

Eleonora nodded.

Ms. Helmchen asked, "Will that be your last trip through *plak fan bonken*?"

"How did you . . ."

Ms. Helmchen cut her off. "The grey mud on your pants, bone dust—it's one of a kind, and I've seen it before . . . on my clothes." She waved a burned hand. "That's how I got this."

Not sure what to say, Eleonora asked, "Why'd you go there?"

Ms. Helmchen sighed. "I suppose the same reason everyone does: someone told me not to."

Eyes on the floor, chewing her lip, Eleonora said, "I wanted to beat the storm."

Ms. Helmchen smiled. "That's a better reason than some."

"Perhaps . . ." Eleonora started, but, not wanting to admit anything, she simply said, "It's late," and left.

She wandered New Skagen for a bit. When she arrived home she stood outside for a moment, wondering what she should say. Her family had expected her home hours ago. She didn't want to lie, but saw no alternative. Some explanation would be required and the truth didn't seem like it would do any good. And tonight Eleonora just didn't feel like being yelled at, boozy hollering whittling away at her, watching Carina deflate in silence, as if that paid for peace. She just wanted to go to bed.

She stepped inside. Carina looked up from her needlepoint. She touched a finger to her lips. Eleonora picked up soft snoring. In the low light of a kerosene lamp she saw her Grandpa passed out on the couch.

Gently closing the door, Eleonora slipped off her shoes and tiptoed to the stairs. A bolt of lightning cracked. The flash and thunder caused Grandpa to sit up. Blinking, he saw her on the stairs.

Smiling, he shouted, "You're home!"

She said flatly, "I got stuck at the station because of the rain."

Getting up, Grandpa looked like someone trying to stand in a wobbly boat. He gestured for her to come over. "Give me a hug."

"I'm all wet."

"Give me a hug, dammit."

She went to him. He squeezed her hard. She gritted her teeth. She could feel blood trickling down her side, leaking from reopened wounds. But he didn't notice.

Patting her roughly on the shoulder he shuffled off towards the basement. The thudding of his feet signaled when he slipped, stumbling down a few steps. Mother and daughter heard him giggling. Carina looked blank, while Eleonora frowned.

Carina got up and closed the basement door. Coming back into the living room she said softly, "You're hurt."

"It's nothing," Eleonora replied.

Carina said, "Do you think he would think so?"

"Are you going to tell him?"

"What? That you went to the place of bones? It wouldn't do any good."

A thought inspired Eleonora to ask, "What makes you say that?"

Sighing, Carina went to the stairs. She gestured for Eleonora to follow. Her daughter hesitated, but did.

They went to Carina's room. In that sepulchral, spartan chamber, Carina went to a small cabinet. She opened a drawer. From under a pile of clothes she produced an old photo. "I should've shown you this a long time ago." Handing the daguerreotype to Eleonora, she said, "That's your aunt Katrijn, my little sister."

The young woman in the photo possessed an infectious grin. Eleonora couldn't help sharing the smile. Katrijn seemed to have been photographed on the verge of laughing.

"Serious faces in photos, she always found them ridiculous. She tried to sit prim and proper, for Mama's sake, but the photographer caught her just in time." Carina's voice caught in her throat. "This is how I like to remember her."

Eleonora handed the picture back. Carina touched the image then buried it in the drawer again.

"You're very much like her. It's almost like she was your mother."

Suspecting the answer, Eleonora asked, "What happened to her?"

"She died. She was a wild child, well, teenager, who went to the place of bones to be alone. Your Grandpa actually thought she was brave, even encouraged her. That lighter he has, that was hers. It was the only way to identify the little they found. He's never been quite the same since. That's why he's the way he is. You remind him of her, so . . . he worries."

Eleonora said, "But I'm not her."

Carina said, "How would you know?" Her eyes watered briefly before something inside her burned them away. "She died long before you arrived." Her mother grimaced. "You only think you know us."

She walked out, leaving Eleonora to shiver in the cold left behind.

·   ·   ·

The next day, Eleonora went back to the courier station. However, with Ms. Helmchen's permission, she acted more as clerk than courier. Two weeks passed. She got along well with customers, even improved the delivery forms. However, anyone with eyes could see the slump in her shoulders when the couriers departed.

One afternoon, no customers around, Ms. Helmchen undid the high collar she wore. Spreading the neck open she sighed, "Much better."

Burns stretched from Ms. Helmchen's chest, reaching like tendrils grasping at her throat. Eleonora tried not to look. Yet, she couldn't help sneaking glances, imagining what the rest of the woman looked like.

Well aware of the peeks, Ms. Helmchen asked, "Do you remember why you wanted this job?"

"I needed the money." Eleonora replied flatly.

"Really?"

Eleonora sighed, adding, "And I wanted to see what's outside of town."

"It's a little scary isn't it?"

"I thought I knew what to expect . . . what to do."

Ms. Helmchen chuckled. "A common mistake nobody ever stops making. We're only prepared after the fact, once everything's gone our way. Success is only in hindsight, and sadly, you'd be surprised what people will call a win." She smiled. "What will be your win, Nora?"

The question haunted her for days. She wondered about the ripples from her aunt. That a person she never knew defined her existence made Eleonora frown. It felt like her life didn't belong to her. Yet, she couldn't deny the pull of the past. After her father died, wrecked by a whipping tail, she had promised to be there for her mother. Lately, she wondered if that pledge meant drowning with Carina. Her mother may have never longed for the abyss, but she seemed to have accepted it.

Then one evening Eleonora came home to the usual cacophony. Grandpa in an apoplectic fit, hollering about cruel gods and the bittersweet depth of his love. She saw Carina at the kitchen window, silently washing dishes, while the old man stormed about the living room shouting and smashing things. It made more sense than usual.

Instead of going inside, Eleonora kept on walking. She followed the coastal road to the fork and without pause marched on into *plak fan bonken*. Even in twilight she easily found the spot where she had fallen, the mammoth spine acting as landmark. She discovered her bike, bent and ruined. Eleonora scooped up the wreckage and carried it out of the place of bones into Reubensville.

She paused only to regard the corpse of the dragon that had chased her. The caw of carrion crows, as well as the smell, made it easy to find. The stink forced her to keep a distance. However, she couldn't help feeling happy for the dragon now at rest, having one last victory chase before the end.

It took a few hours to get to Sander Hagen's shop, but time seemed limitless to her now.

Showing him the cycle, she asked, "Can you fix this?"

He nodded. "Of course, though, honestly, this is a mess. It would probably be better to start from scratch."

She smiled. "In that case, I have some ideas for improvements."

"A better design?"

"Yes."

"Go on," Sander said, beaming at the prospect of innovation.

·   ·   ·

Sometimes life is like riding a bicycle downhill. The speed is suddenly faster than expected, and there are only two options: brake or pedal on. Eleonora never planned on braking again.

A week after explaining her concept to Sander, Eleonora came downstairs. She found Carina at the stove, quietly preparing breakfast. Her Grandpa sat at the kitchen table, his arms crossed, and a scowl on his face.

No longer in a mood to baby his hangover foulness, Eleonora said brightly, "Good morning."

"Good morning," Carina almost whispered.

Grandpa nodded. "Is it good?"

"What else would it be?" Eleonora said. She sniffed the aroma of warming flapjacks, hugged her mother, and said, "Smells great."

Grandpa said, "Would you care to explain something?"

"What?"

He reached into a shirt pocket, "This letter was in the box. A night courier delivered it." Unfolding a crumpled ball he read, "'Dear Ms. Rask, I've completed the cycle according to your specifications. It should be capable of going off-road. You'll be able to ride anywhere now. Please pick it up at your convenience.' What's this?"

Eleonora replied, "It's my business."

"Your business is my business."

"No, it's . . ."

He cut her off, "If you leave the road that's only wilderness—no place for a little girl."

"I'm twenty years old."

"You should thank God I'm here to stop whatever this foolishness is."

Swallowing hard, Eleonora said, "I don't, and you can't."

Grandpa slammed his fist on the table, knocking a glass over. Its contents spilled out. His eyes bulging in rage, he watched it roll over the edge, fall, and shatter.

Eleonora said, "I'm leaving."

"The hell you are!" Grandpa roared.

Carina said, "She's right."

They looked at Carina as she calmly plated pancakes. Carrying the loaded plate, she stepped between the two.

Speaking softly, Carina said, "It's time for her to go. She'll be back when she gets back. Isn't that right?"

Eleonora nodded. "I'll be home."

"We'll see you then," her mother said. Serving Grandpa breakfast, Carina added, speaking over his grumbling, "I'll get your bag."

Silently, her mother went upstairs. She returned shortly carrying a satchel full of clothes and a few other items. She handed it to her daughter.

Smiling slightly, Carina said, "Go."

Throwing the satchel over one shoulder, Eleonora rushed outside. She could feel a part of herself insisting she go back, offer a proper thanks and goodbye, but she feared any hesitation now risked getting stuck. So she ran, recalling Carina's words: "You only think you know us."

She ran through the place of bones, walked the streets of Reubensville, and strolled breathless into Sander's shop. The trip took most of the day, but only felt like minutes. Sander showed her the bike. Eleonora glowed.

"What do I owe you?" she asked.

"Just let me keep me making more. I really think others will want this. This could bring a little life back to this sleepy shop. I'll share the profits, of course."

She said, "I don't know when I'll be back this way."

"When you come back, your money will be here."

She nodded. Getting on the bike, she pedaled off.

Sander called out, "Where are you going?"

Eleonora grinned.

"Wherever I want to."

Cycling out of Reubensville, cruising the coastal road, she reached out for the horizon. It did lie out of reach, but now she could chase it. So Eleonora rode.

'ROUND

J. A. Sabangan

As Rain pedaled down the road, her skirts rippling with the wind, hair whipping this way and that, the sunlight finally arrived. She let go of the handlebar to stroke Petya, who was curled around her neck. His smooth scales lightly scraped her bare skin.

After what seemed like endless drizzling, today was the first day they could go on a proper ride, unhurried and without fuss. Which meant her companion was quickly getting bored.

When he'd had enough of the lolling pace, he launched from his perch straight up toward the clouds.

After a glance around to see if anyone was watching, Rain chuckled in delight as he beat his wings, circling around her until he matched pace. As Petya ducked into Rain's shadow, the young woman rang her bell twice, nodding at their neighbor from across the street two houses down.

The man raised his newspaper from the porch swing and, for a fleeting moment, Rain saw the resemblance he had to his parents.

She'd taken the same route for ten years, from the time she turned eight, the hem of her skirts flying toward her shoulders, boasting the yellow sports shorts beneath. Her legs would pump with enthusiasm, faster and faster. Zipping down the street, then back up, then around and around and around the garden. Her garden.

The sunflowers slowly waved in the breeze, and she'd reach out a hand to wave back. The fragrance of the lilies would waft from the fountain, her favorite part of the property, the gurgling centerpiece. Warm sunshine kissed her nose and cheeks, leaving their light pink stain behind.

Petya was too young to fly then, having only just hatched from his sturdy scaly home. "Where'd you get this?" Rain had asked her grandmother. Nanay Luz just pat her head before attending to the guest waiting in the healing room. During those first few months, he sat contentedly in the wicker basket, blowing hot puffs of breath on Rain's knuckles when he could stand long enough before tumbling back down.

The man was younger then, too, returning from law school to care for his elderly parents, the same ones who'd smiled in greeting as she rode past, commenting after her when they thought she couldn't hear.

"Sweet girl, that one. Lovely, but peculiar."

"They're a little strange, that family of hers."

Or even, "I wonder why they don't just go back to their country."

At home, when she'd ask her mother what they meant, Xian would say, "'Peculiar' is a word people use when they have no other way to describe another person's brilliance." Petya had snorted in agreement.

"But I'm *not* different. They have the same color hair!" Rain insisted, grabbing fistfuls of her wispy silver strands. Yet her fervor melted just as quickly. "What's wrong with me? Am I—Am I—" Rain had hiccuped before she could finish.

Xian had drawn her daughter close, holding young Rain's chin between her thumb and forefinger. "You are my daughter, and you are *extraordinary*. Some people might see your face, your skin, and question these parts of you. But just like sampaguita, kalachuchi, and bougainvillea are flowers of different shapes, colors, and sizes, our family—you, me, Nanay Luz—and our neighbor's family are all people of different shapes, colors, and sizes. "She stroked her daughter's hair. "Never mind what they say. Ride in your gorgeous skirts and race with the wind. Be as free as I know your spirit to be. Their words reflect outdated beliefs. Besides," she paused to look Rain in the eye. "Their ideas will soon die with them."

This echoed in Rain's mind when, not a year later, the couple passed on.

Rain pedaled slower. Through the years, she still wore skirts when she rode into the city, pants and jeans never suiting her the way they did the neighborhood folk. Even in the winter, she wore skirts without stockings.

The familiar whirring of the two wheels beneath her mimicked her mind, the thought of the long deceased couple taking turns in her subconscious, even as she acknowledged each person on the sidewalk.

Though no one spoke, she could see it. The same look. A wrinkle at the corners of their eyes, a slight shake of their heads. *All the same*, Rain noted. Petya had since alighted back on her shoulder, not wanting to draw unwarranted attention, anchoring himself across her collarbone, making a full loop with his tail tucked into the corner of his mouth. He swayed side to side as Rain rode on.

Despite the smiles, she felt their thoughts as they gazed around the frame of her face before snapping back to meet her eyes.

Peculiar, the tick of their head seemed to imply.

But Xian's voice cut through. *You are my daughter, and you are extraordinary.*

"What if I'm not, though? What if I'm just a freak?" Rain said aloud, Petya hanging on. Listening. "What if . . ." The words lingered in the air before she nodded at the next passerby. Another tilt, another double take.

When her destination drew close, a genuine smile replaced the polite one. Next to the garden, this was her other favorite place on earth.

Climbing off the metal frame she sauntered through the door, chimes announcing her arrival.

As the young man behind the tall glass display greeted her, Rain saw him already stuffing a brioche into a paper bag. He knew what she'd ask for. Her order never changed.

"Hey, Rain! Nice scarf. It's so bright and"—a pause to scratch at patchy stubble—"voluminous."

Rain touched the iridescent scales as Petya quietly huffed on her neck in appreciation.

"Thanks, Jason. My . . . scarf was given to me by my grandmother years ago. I'm sure she's proud I'm taking good care of her . . . scarf."

"I mean, it kinda looks like how I'd imagine a fire drake would. If only they were real!"

"That'd be pretty awesome, huh?" Rain smirked as Petya blew silent bursts of hot air.

Whatever thoughts Rain had entered with, she let them slide from her mind, off her back, and onto the ground.

"How is your grandmother?" Jason asked, handing her not one but two pastry bags. Rain's smile widened, but before she could answer, he continued. "Will you be training with her soon?"

"I—" A blink. Then another. No one had ever asked her that before. "I don't know."

He gave her a knowing grin. "Don't want to follow her footsteps?"

"No, I do!" she cut in, perhaps too quickly. "I do," she said softly, then added, "But I don't think I'd be any good." One hand fiddled with the ends of her hair.

"What do you mean? If you want to be a healer, be a healer. As far as I can tell, you'd be amazing."

Rain stroked Petya, whose warm breath tickled her neck. "What makes you say that?"

Jason rubbed at his stubble.

"Okay, this'll sound a little weird, but hear me out, ok?" When she nodded, he continued. "Your hands"—her cocked eyebrow, his gestures a *hold on, let me explain*—"Remember band camp in elementary, Red Rover?"

"Yeah?"

"That time the Smith brothers mauled us, practically tearing out my shoulder—"

A shared wince. "Those boys were the worst."

"They were. But when you touched my arm, seeing if I was all right, well, your hands were so warm—I kinda felt better."

Waving as if to erase his statement, Rain said, "You're imagining things."

"And that time freshman year, racing downhill at Oaks Park, no handlebars?"

Rain burst out laughing. "Your mom got so mad!"

"All the blood—I was a mess." Jason shook his head. "But you put your arm around me while we waited for my parents, rubbing my back, feeling for broken bones, I felt—"

"Better?" She was teasing him, but his words tugged her.

"Yeah."

They looked at each other, taking turns smiling and shaking their heads. After a breath, Rain lifted the pastry bags as Jason waved at her, the bells tinkling behind her.

Riding back home, the sunshine mild, snippets of the conversation mingled with the memories. At a traffic light, a pedestrian caught her attention.

"Hey," the young lady said.

A quick nod before pushing off at the flash of green.

But the lady persisted. "Is your hair dyed?"

"No," Rain replied, looking back.

"I love it!" The wind carried the words to Rain's ears.

Stunned, she kept going.

Peculiar was just another word to describe brilliance. Not a limitation, but a detail that might not have any bearing on anything. Maybe she could be the healer she'd dreamt of becoming but never allowed herself to admit out loud.

As the familiar twists and turns came into sight, Rain shook her head to let the silver reflect the sunlight back out into the world. Or, at least, to the passersby around her.

People were just people, and they had their beliefs.

Whatever they thought—positive, negative, neither—eventually, their ideas will die with them.

BICYCLE ART

C.G. Beckman

One summer evening, a young man coasted along a quiet street of row houses in DC, heading to a house party. Beside him, his friend, likewise coasting, likewise without hands. They talked, as they often did, about dating. Suddenly pensive, the young man asked his friend, "Have you ever been in love?"

His friend thrust his hands into his jacket pockets and sucked in his breath.

"Sure," he said. They carved through an empty intersection, the traffic light flashing. "But I mean, what do you mean, 'in love'? Like, my girlfriend in college, I don't think I'll ever love like that again. But you know the story—she left me for that Norwegian guy, Sven, after studying abroad."

"Ha . . . right. Sven." He imagined the ex-girlfriend living with Sven in Oslo, perhaps this very night curled up on a piece of elegant mid-century furniture, reading Scandinavian noir novels while the Northern Lights play outside their window.

The wind pulled a single tear from a corner of the young man's eye. "I don't think I've ever really been in love," he said.

What he did not realize was that he lived under a curse placed on him long ago. Fifteen years earlier, while riding his bicycle down a hill on his way to buy the latest Radiohead CD, he had nearly knocked over a diminutive older man wrapped in a shawl. The man had been about to cross the street with a cheerful and companionable miniature Xolo, a Mexican hairless dog named *El Dragón*, so-named because of his whiskers, like the drooping mustache of a dragon puppet on Chinese New Year, and his hand-knitted wool vests in green diamond patterns that suggested dragon scales. Though generally very alert, the dog was, at that moment, looking the other way, toward a dachshund on the other side of the road. This man was a gifted herbalist, possessed a sharp wit, and cultivated a generous heart. But that evening he was in the grip of a nagging pain in his lower-right molar, and his daughter in Montreal had just called to complain about her marriage, which seemed headed for divorce after all.

The young fellow had not seen him until he emerged from between the parked cars. As he swerved to avoid him, his backpack swung out to the side and brushed the man's shoulder. It spun him sideways. The sudden and unexpected attack on his person made him so viscerally angry that he thrust a finger out from under the shawl and yelled in French, in a voice that began as a rumble and ended as a howl, "As long as you ride that bike, may you remain wholly un-enamored by your lovers!"

But the young fellow was already a good distance away, moving as he was, very quickly down the hill. Though he heard each word clearly, he spoke no French, and was none the wiser to the import of the old man's exclamation.

The young men rode around a circle with a fountain in the middle. The young man rode a green Schwinn—the same bike he'd been riding that day, fifteen years ago, on the hill and had ridden nearly every day since.

"Everybody loves differently," said his friend. "I bet you've been in love, you just didn't recognize it."

The young man didn't think so. He was pretty sure he'd never loved any woman, truly.

"Who knows?" his friend said. "Maybe she'll be at the party tonight."

Yeah, thought the young man sarcastically, who knows?

•   •   •

"What are you doing, Wilma? That doesn't look safe!"

Wilma pushed the soldering mask up onto her forehead and the high-pitched screech of the electric hacksaw died away. She turned to greet her roommate, a mischievous smile spreading on her freckled face. It was late morning and the sun had warmed the street in front of their small row house enough that she had cast off her sweatshirt.

"Some idiot left their bike locked to our front gate last night, so . . . I'm sawing off the lock."

Wilma's roommate was impressed. It was a dramatic measure, but then Wilma had a knack for the dramatic. A sculptor and a carpenter, she was a hands-on kind of woman.

Twelve hours earlier, their living room had been filled with the buzz of voices. A party had been underway, and one of those sudden elevations in decibel level had just happened; everyone shouted to be heard. There was plenty of beer left in the keg, and a fresh order of pizza had just arrived.

Wilma had been talking to a guy who she was starting to think she might want to have a drink with sometime, just the two of them. He was handsome in an unconventional way and seemed entirely himself. They talked, for some reason, about an obscure Beach Boys song from when the group was doing comparatively more drugs than during earlier albums. He started shout-singing a line, and she finished it. She was a little tone-deaf, but she sang with such gusto that they both laughed.

Wilma's roommate had appeared beside them, and made her presence felt, apologetically but insistently. The pizza guy needed a cash tip. Wilma said to our guy, "I'll be right back . . . don't go anywhere!"

She tipped the delivery guy, and intended to return to the living room, but was intercepted by several newly-arrived friends from whose greetings she could not extricate herself too quickly. By the time she returned, the young man had disappeared. She asked her roommate where he'd gone and she pointed vaguely to the kitchen. No sign of him there either.

The next morning, as steam rose from a mug beside her laptop, Wilma wrote a quick note and pasted it on Facebook:

> A poem to the owner of the green Schwinn locked to my garden gate:
>
> *I buzz-sawed your lock; your bike was blocking the walk;*
>
> *And, as I noticed some rust on the frame and the chain*
>
> *I'm of half a mind to have it soar to new heights,*
>
> *In my sculpture, entitled "Bicycle Dragon Takes Flight."*

Over the next few days, the slapdash poem garnered a few wry comments and a dozen likes, but no one claimed the bicycle.

The day after the party, the young man had gone straight from work to the airport for a two-week trip to the Caribbean island of Martinique. He'd asked his friend to get the extra bike key from his apartment and retrieve the bike, but his friend hadn't responded. Distracted by the beach, introductory French lessons, and patchy internet connections, he'd put the bike out of his mind.

He saw the Facebook post when he got back two weeks later, brought into his feed through a mutual friend on a Sunday afternoon as he took a taxi back from the airport. Rather than message her, he decided on a whim to have the driver change course and deliver him to Wilma's front door.

·   ·   ·

Wilma paused for a moment in the narrow backyard that doubled as an open-air workshop, trying to decide if she should really destroy someone's obviously well-loved bicycle. Then she shrugged, and, figuring that the sculpture would be worth more than the bike, hacksawed the frame in two. She removed the chain and hung it from the handlebars. After a few coats of gold and green spray paint, it would work beautifully for the new installation she was doing for the yupster bike store down the street.

A door opened, and she heard her roommate's voice: ". . . she's out here, I think."

Wilma looked up and saw the young man stepping on to the back deck.

"I remember you!" Wilma exclaimed. She wiped the grease on her hands onto her jeans. "From the party, right? We sang the 'vegetables' song together!"

"Yeah, that's right!" he laughed. He gestured at the pieces of his bicycle, with a put-on smile. "So, what are you up to?"

He tried to mask the nearly visceral pain he felt in seeing his bike of fifteen years cut into two and arranged in pieces on the ground.

"Oh my god! You're not . . ."

"Yeah," he chuckled, awkwardly, "I was the guy with the bike. Sorry it took me so long to come by."

Wilma apologized profusely, but he waved a hand.

Before him was a picture of loveliness: the woman's hair was tied loosely across her left shoulder, and there were smears of grease across her face and hands. He found, quite suddenly, that he no longer cared about the bicycle.

·   ·   ·

Two months later, they walked hand-in-hand on her street in the late evening, after watching coverage of the presidential elections at a bar. A tinge of color still clung to the clouds above, though it was early November. They joked and laughed, reveling in the evening's buzz and the anticipation of the few hours ahead before sleep.

In front of them in the dusky darkness tottered a small figure wrapped in a shawl. He was walking a small dog in a knitted green vest that looked very much like the scaly armor of a dragon. As the young man and Wilma passed him beneath a streetlamp, they saw the kindly face of an old man looking up at them. He smiled, met their eyes very briefly, and made a gentle salutation of two raised fingers. He spoke softly, in French, as they passed.

"Enchanted, together. May you always remain so."

His words were too soft and indistinct for their ears, but they could hear that they were French, and, conscious that the words conveyed something friendly, they giggled, and called back to him: "Bonne nuit, Monsieur!"

Their fingers brushed the neighbor's rose bushes as they turned into the front gate. They walked upstairs to Wilma's room, from where the young man, standing at the window for a moment, could see the sculpture, half-finished yet already formidable. Spokes had been twisted into flaring nostrils, and metallic claws welded to a wheel rim, which caught the wind and turned, quickly and silently, glinting in the moonlight.

SIMPLE TREASURE

J.A. Gross

Kia breathes out, warming the metal, then shaping it with her fingers. It cools slowly beneath her touch, letting her make the join with ease. Too much and the metal will melt. Too little and it won't hold. Balance is the optimal solution, especially given what her creation will be used for.

This bike was made to climb. Fast and strong; made for a client who preferred the tried and true to newer carbon fibers. Kia licks a finger then draws a slow path around the seam, leaving behind the raised curlicue that is her signature. This is the moment of pleasure. Drawing to the end of a project. Steel beast beneath her fingers needing only paint and the customer's own preferences to bring it fully to life.

The tinkling doorbell catches her attention. Kia is careful to draw her fire back down into her fingers, rubbing them on her apron to speed their cooling.

"Can I help you?"

Her newest customer looks up from beneath a harried brow, pushing her thick, kinky curly hair behind one ear. "Yes, please. I need . . . I mean, my daughter. She needs a bicycle. A friend told me about your place; she has one of yours and really loves it. She said maybe you could help me."

Help. "Perhaps," Kia says. Her customer can't see how she tastes the air with whiskers that are so fine that they can't be seen by the naked eye. A weariness hangs on this woman that is close kin to desperation. There's more to her than meets the eye. Stepping forward, Kia lifts the hinged counter and beckons the woman to come into her lair. "Right this way."

Sometimes, if they are weary enough or just more in tune to the world around them, a person can sense the creature that lives beneath Kia's benign skin. For the most part, people see what they wish to see: a tall, brown-skinned woman with muscular forearms. Head shaved clean and covered with a worn bandana. Her hands, calloused and work worn. Hundreds of years ago, there wasn't a forge that would even consider letting Kia near metal. Working with it was considered unseemly for a woman, no matter that she'd forgotten more metal lore than most humans had known in their somewhat insignificant lifespans. She knew patience, letting anger cool to an ember while she waited for those who guarded human-created gates to die off.

The customer brushed by, tote bag clutched to her side, whispering thanks.

"My daughter, Alicia, she really wants a bike. To ride to school with her friends," the woman says, looking at the bikes that surrounded them. "I don't have a lot of money but my friend said that you might have something used that's been fixed up. Hopefully I can get her something like that for now and when things get better, something a little newer."

It's not the first time Kia's heard this plea, which is why she keeps the stash in the back of the shop. Gently used bikes that need either a little attention or a full rebuild. Affordability is key, which is something her clutch mates mock her for. "It's your hoard," they'd said to her more than once. "Why would you ever let something like that out of your sight?"

Why indeed?

"Your daughter," Kia says. "How tall is she? What colors does she like?" As they converse, she walks around the room, touching each bike, feeling them stir with the little bit of magic she's imbued in each one. They are plain yet proud vehicles, refurbished with just as much care as one of the builds in the front. They have purpose and are willing to live it out with the right person. Finally, one leaps to the fore of her attention—mid-sized, cinnamon red with sturdy, reliable tires.

The woman stands by her side and smiles hesitantly. "That one, maybe. Yes," she says even more firmly. "That's the one."

Kia nods and pulls it forward. "$100.00."

The woman is taken aback. "Are you sure? I can pay some more." She digs into her bag and pulls up a wad of bills. "I don't want to take advantage." The desperation is mixed with fierce pride.

Kia shrugs. "You're daughter is growing. Doesn't make much sense to charge you a lot when you'll probably be back here in a year." She runs a finger over the handle bar, urging a tiny bit more heat into the bike. She raises age-old eyes to her customer. "$100.00 is more than enough."

A worn one hundred dollar bill sits in Kia's apron pocket once the deal is struck. The bike gives a little shimmy as it's wheeled out of the shop and on its way to its new owner. Turning the sign to 'closed', she stretches then breathes out, warming the air around her. Her eyes run over frames, wheels, and handlebars until it alights on a dull blue bike tucked in a corner. Kia crooks a finger and it rolls out slowly on flat tires. "You'll do," she says kindly, resting her hand on the rusted handlebar. "You'll be ready when she comes back."

CONTRIBUTORS

Paul Abbamondi is a caffeine-dependent life form living in New Jersey. He likes puns, cats, drawing comics, and writing short stories. Please write to him at pdabbamondi@gmail.com because he also likes emails.

· · ·

As a kid, C.G. Beckman often rode his coaster brake bicycle along the Potomac River. More recently, he spent six months commuting in Pune, India on a steel frame bicycle. He now works as a lawyer at a medium-sized federal agency, and belongs to an inspiring writing group.

· · ·

Joyce Chng lives in Singapore. Their fiction has appeared in *The Apex Book of World SF II*, *We See A Different Frontier*, *Cranky Ladies of History*, and *Accessing The Future*. Joyce also co-edited *THE SEA IS OURS: Tales of Steampunk Southeast Asia* with Jaymee Goh. Their recent space opera novels deal with wolf clans (*Starfang: Rise of the Clan*) and vineyards (*Water into Wine*) respectively. They also write speculative poetry with recent ones in *Rambutan Literary* and *Uncanny Magazine*. Occasionally, they wrangle article editing at *Strange Horizons* and *Umbel & Panicle*, a poetry journal about and for plants and botany. Alter-ego J. Damask writes about werewolves in Singapore. You can find them at awolfstale.wordpress.com and @jolantru on Twitter. (Pronouns: she/her, they/their).

· · ·

Phil Cowhig is a lifelong science and science-fiction enthusiast. He lives in the UK with his family, shelves of books and DVDs, and slightly too many bicycles. This is his first work of fiction for about 30 years.

· · ·

Monique Cuillerier lives in Ottawa with her partner, children (when they're home from university), and animals. Her flash fiction has appeared in the last two Queer Sci Fi anthologies, *Impact* and *Migration*. She writes fiction, long and short, when she is not procrastinating on Twitter at @MoniqueAC or sporadically posting at notwhereilive.ca.

· · ·

J.A. Gross is a fifty-something Black lesbian making life in Oakland, California, with her wife and her cat. A long time prose and non-fiction writer, her work has appeared in *Luna Station Quarterly* and a variety of other publications including *Our Bodies, Our Bikes* (Microcosm Publishing).

· · ·

Tessa Hulls is an artist/writer/adventurer who fuses her bike travel and creative practice in unorthodox ways. She's currently working on a nonfiction graphic novel exploring mixed race identity, loss of culture, mother/daughter relationships and the American fascination with the frontier as told through the life story of her maternal grandmother, Sun Yi. www.tessahulls.com @tessahulls

· · ·

Gretchin Lair is a pretend patient, creative advocate and novice enchantivist. She believes in kindness, curiosity, compassion and consent. She sings to herself when she's sure nobody can hear. You can contact her at gretchin@scarletstarstudios.com.

•   •   •

M. Lopes da Silva is an author and fine artist living in Los Angeles. Her short fiction has appeared in a variety of publications, from *Mad Scientist Journal*'s *Utter Fabrication* anthology, to the upcoming *Nightscript Vol. IV*. She is currently working on her upcoming science fiction thriller, *The Somniferri*, as well as a weird western novella titled *On a Dead Horse*. She blogs at mlopesdasilva.wordpress.com

•   •   •

Taru Luojola is a Finnish writer and translator who, because of their Finnishness, casually calls everyone 'them'. Their first velopunk novel, a political satire set in the fictitious country of Bataranam, was published in Finland in 2018. "Beasts of Bataranam" is their first velopunk story originally written in English.

•   •   •

Kate Macdonald is a writer, publisher, editor, academic researcher and literary historian. She lives and works in Bath, in the UK.

•   •   •

Alice Pow is a transgender lesbian and a cyborgian pile of electric meat who writes prose, poetry, and everything in between. Her work has previously appeared in *Black Elephant*, Bradley University's *Broadside, 200ccs: Year One*, and *Meet Cute Mag*. Find her on Twitter @AlicePow8.

•   •   •

J. Rohr is a Chicago native with a taste for history, and wandering the city at odd hours. He writes the blog www.honestyisnotcontagious.com in order to deal with the more corrosive aspects of everyday life.

•   •   •

Jennifer Lee Rossman has never ridden a bicycle but she does have a wicked cool wheelchair. She is a queer, autistic, and disabled science fiction writer from Binghamton, New York. Follow her on Twitter @JenLRossman

•   •   •

J. A. Sabangan is a multi-passionate who writes and dances to her heart's content. Currently living in Portland, OR, she indulges in chocolate and coffee in equal measure. You can learn more about her urban fantasy novels as well as other works at HintofJam. com or on Instagram and Twitter @xoxJamae.

•   •   •

Sarena Ulibarri is a graduate of the Clarion Fantasy and Science Fiction Writers' Workshop at UCSD, and earned an MFA from the University of Colorado, Boulder. Her fiction has appeared in magazines such as *Lightspeed* and *Fantastic Stories of the Imagination*, as well as anthologies such as *Dear Robot: An Anthology of Epistolary Science Fiction* and *Biketopia: Feminist Bicycle Science Fiction Stories in Extreme Futures*. Find more at SarenaUlibarri.com.

SUBSCRIBE TO EVERYTHING WE PUBLISH!

Do you love what Microcosm publishes?

Do you want us to publish more great stuff?

Would you like to receive each new title as it's published?

Subscribe as a BFF to our new titles and we'll mail them all to you as they are released!

$13-30/mo, pay what you can afford!

microcosmpublishing.com/bff